Molly Perry

Copyright © 2012 by Molly Perry.

Library of Congress Control Number: 2012916540
ISBN: Hardcover   978-1-4797-1284-7
               Softcover   978-1-4797-1283-0
               Ebook   978-1-4797-1285-4

All rights reserved. No part of this book may be reproduced or transmitted in any form or by any means, electronic or mechanical, including photocopying, recording, or by any information storage and retrieval system, without permission in writing from the copyright owner.

This is a work of fiction. Names, characters, places and incidents either are the product of the author's imagination or are used fictitiously, and any resemblance to any actual persons, living or dead, events, or locales is entirely coincidental.

This book was printed in the United States of America.

To order additional copies of this book, contact:
Xlibris Corporation
1-888-795-4274
www.Xlibris.com
Orders@Xlibris.com
112518

Acknowledgments

I would like to thank my husband Steve Perry for patiently supporting me on this and any other writing project I have worked on.

I want to thank all those members of the late Marcie Anderson's Writer's group, especially Liz Vollstadt, Donna Peltz and Martha Thorp who listened to each chapter and all the rewrites when I began the process of writing this book.

Thanks to my son, David Firestone, my brother Paul Cohen, sister-in-law Risa Cohen and my late step-son J.J. Perry for believing in me as a writer and encouraging me to keep writing.

Thanks to my brother Garry Cohen for reading many drafts of this story and giving me much helpful feedback.

Thanks to the many third graders who have listened to the story over the last ten plus years and who have relentlessly begged for a published copy.

I want to thank my current writer's group, The Heights Writers, especially Beth Choi and Kevin McMahon, who give me great feedback and encouragement.

Thanks to Xlibris for believing in this book and guiding me through the process of publishing it.

Thanks to Sylvia Masek. She is a wonderful artist/illustrator who did a wonderful job bringing my characters and story to life.

In memory of Kelly Alexis Firestone.

Chapter 1

"CAN I HAVE a look at The Game?" asked Jimmy. "I want to show Jamal and Lilly."

"Jimmy, this is the third time in three days that you've come to see The Game," said Dad. He took off his glasses and rubbed his eyes with his fingers. Dad looked bone tired.

"OK, Son, but just for a little while. I've got an appointment with Mr. Avery at the Matterhorn Loan Company. I can only hope that he can help keep the children's museum from shutting down before it even has a chance to get started."

Dad walked over to the room that had once been the gym and-meeting room in a small elementary school, which had been standing empty for many years. Soon, if Dad could get the loan from Mr. Avery, the little school would be transformed into the Mayville Children's Museum.

Right now, the room was crammed with boxes and crates filled with all sorts of items that would turn the building into a place for children to learn and explore.

Dad unlocked a medium-sized wooden crate and very carefully pulled out a beautiful mahogany box with a game board inlaid in gold on the top. The words "The Game" were carved in swirls and curlicues on one side of the box.

Dad whistled softly. "What a beautiful old game," he said. "I can't believe Mrs. Pennyman would actually donate it to the museum. She told me that it has been in her family for many generations."

Jimmy rubbed his hand ever so lightly over the game board. He gently pulled out the drawer from one of the sides and looked down at the play money, tokens, and cards. Jimmy then closed the drawer with care.

Dad put his hand on Jimmy's shoulder and gave it a squeeze. "You and that game," Dad said with a sigh. "What is it that makes you come every day for a look?"

Ten-year-old Jimmy, like Dad, was thin with brown wavy hair and serious brown eyes that could not be hidden behind wire-rimmed glasses.

Jimmy shrugged his shoulders, never taking his eyes off the shiny mahogany box. "I don't know . . . I just like it."

"C'mon, Dad," said Lilly, Jimmy's thirteen-year-old sister. Lilly chewed her gum and checked her fingernails for even the slightest chip. "Everybody knows that since last summer, Jimmy has been crazy about playing board games." Lilly gave her curly red hair a shake and smoothed her capri pants and matching top outfit.

"She's right, Mr. Stone," said Jamal, Jimmy's friend, who lives across the street. "Don't you remember last July when I brought over my stack of board games? The rain wouldn't stop, and we were bored out of our minds. We ended up having a four-day game-playing marathon."

"Yeah, and Jimmy hasn't stopped playing since," said Lilly, cracking her gum loudly to make the point. "It's really embarrassing when my friends come over. There is my younger brother sitting in his room playing one of his nonstop games by himself."

Lilly rolled her eyes. "He doesn't even care if he has real people playing with him . . . He just plays as if people were there. In one game, I think he even has all the spaces memorized and how much you have to pay to land on them. How weird is that?"

"Anyone can jump in a game and play anytime they want," said Jimmy, defending himself.

Lilly and Jamal looked at each other and started to laugh. "Sure, Jimmy," said Jamal, popping one of his mini-chocolate and caramel candies into his mouth. "But then after they make a few deals with you, somehow they're broke!"

Dad shook his head and laughed a low, tired laugh. He stuck his hand in his pocket and pulled out some keys and tossed them to Lilly. "You're the eldest, Lilly. Please lock up when you're all finished looking at The Game."

"Great. First, Mom makes me bring Jimmy over here to get him out of the house, and now I have to be a babysitter for him and Jamal while you leave. This taking responsibility thing is really getting old. Is this how my whole summer vacation is going to be?"

"It's important, Lilly," answered Dad. "Thirteen is old enough to know that. The children's museum has been in the making for a long time. It has been my dream to make a museum where children can learn about the past and the present-day world. They can learn by touching, by doing experiments, or by just having fun playing games. However, at the moment, I have no more money to continue getting it started. Today, I'm hoping to get some help."

"Dad, if you get money from the loan company, would that also mean we could stay in our house?" asked Jimmy. "Lilly and I don't want to move to the small apartment house across the street. We don't want to look out the window and watch other kids playing in our yard."

"Don't you know that your mother and I want to stay in the house too?" softly responded Dad with tears welling up in his eyes. "The loan would definitely help keep us in our house and keep the museum alive."

Dad wiped his eyes. And then with a sudden smile, he looked at them. A little spark flashed for a moment in his eyes. "One can only hope."

Lilly rolled her eyes for the second time. "There is never enough money for the museum. We hear you and Mom talking about it all the time."

"How much money do you need?" Jimmy asked as Dad was walking toward the front door.

"We need a lot," said Dad, stopping in front of the aquarium that hummed quietly in the corner. He took a moment to look at the beautiful fish swimming contentedly around the tank without a bit of worry about the museum's money problems.

"We need more than twenty thousand dollars." Dad mumbled to himself as he walked out the door. But Jimmy, Lilly, and Jamal managed to hear. They looked at each other with their mouths open.

Lilly shook her head. "What Dad really needs is a magic wand!"

It wasn't even five minutes after Dad left the museum that Jimmy let Lilly and Jamal in on his big secret.

Chapter 2

"WHAT A STRANGE and cool-looking game," said Jamal, chewing away on another mini-bite candy as he looked closely at The Game. His round face, the color of caramel, was covered with freckles, which seemed to slide to the sides of his face whenever he was chewing on a mouthful of some goodie or another.

"Check out the boxes that are around the edges of the game board. What do they mean? It looks like street names and other places. Let's see—there are airports, railroads, parking garage, city hall, courthouse, bank, city park . . ."

"It's interesting you should notice," said Jimmy, interrupting Jamal. "There is something I need to tell you guys."

"What now, Jimmy?" asked Lilly. "Did you play The Game when Dad wasn't looking? Did you break something? Oh great! I bet you did. Now I'm going to get into trouble because I am supposed to keep an eye on you."

"Can I trust you guys with a big secret?" asked Jimmy, completely ignoring Lilly's comments.

Jamal's eyes got big as he stared at Jimmy. "I guess so," he said nervously and began cramming another mini-bite into his already full mouth.

"Spill, Jimmy," said Lilly, "so we can fix whatever is wrong and get out of here. I'm supposed to be at my friend's house in a few hours, and since we can't afford a cell phone anymore, I can't call her to let her know I will be late."

Jamal tried to chew, swallow, and talk all at the same time. "Wait . . . Jimmy . . . did you . . . by any chance . . . play with this game? Is that what you are going to tell us?"

"Yes, a little," Jimmy answered.

"What do you mean a little?" asked Lilly. "I swear, Jimmy, if you broke something, you are going to be the one in trouble, not me."

"Just tell us, Jimmy," said Jamal softly with a slight quiver in his voice.

"Well . . . the first time I looked at The Game, I started to set it up to play, which was tricky because I couldn't find the directions and . . . well . . ."

"Well . . . what?" Lilly and Jamal asked together.

Jimmy didn't answer with words. Instead, he lifted the lid off the beautiful wooden box.

"Jimmy! Stop! That top isn't supposed to come off! Please don't do it!" Lilly begged.

Jimmy ignored her as he carefully put the top aside while Jamal and Lilly bumped heads, leaning over to look inside.

"Look! You can see the drawer with the tokens, money, and cards," said Jamal.

"What's this?" asked Lilly, pointing to a small space next to the drawer. Without waiting for an answer, Lilly reached in and pulled out a token from the beautiful blue velvet-lined space next to the drawer. It was a token that they had never seen in any game before.

"Wow!" Jamal said with disbelief. "Look! The token is an exact copy of your Dad's museum. It even has the sign that your Mom painted and hung by the front door. See, the sign says, Mayville Children's Museum."

Lilly looked at Jimmy and then down at the token. "How can this be?"

"I wish I knew," said Jimmy. "But we better put it back."

Lilly put the museum token back in the velvet-lined space and Jimmy replaced the top of the box.

"Anyway, I was beginning to set The Game up when Dad called me from the back office and told me it was time to go. So I quickly put the cards, tokens, and money back before he had a chance to see them."

"You mean Dad doesn't know about the museum token?" asked Lilly.

"I don't think so," said Jimmy. "But I doubt that he'd be interested right now—with all his money worries."

"So let's take out the cards, tokens, and money," Jamal exclaimed. "Let's play!"

A smile crept across Jimmy's face and his eyes sparkled.

"OK!" he said. And in a flash, out came the contents of the side drawer of The Game. First, Jimmy passed out some money to each person. Then, he put the stack of red cards in a square that was marked "red cards" near the middle of the game board.

Next, he took out another stack of yellow cards that matched some of the boxes that went all the way around the game board. He put the yellow cards in another box on the board marked properties.

Finally, Jimmy picked up some of the tokens and put them in his hand. "Which one do you want?" he asked.

"What a cute little 'wiener dog,'" said Jamal, picking the dachshund token.

"I guess I'll take the pink mini-bus," said Lilly. "Look, it's got flowers all over it."

"Then I will take the king's crown," said Jimmy.

They quickly put their tokens on "Start."

"Let's roll!" said Jamal.

"OMG! I hope this doesn't get me in trouble," said Lilly, but by looking at her smile, anyone could tell she was excited to play.

"OK, Jamal, you're first, but roll the dice on the floor. I don't want to scratch up the board," Jimmy explained.

Jamal moved the little wiener dog. "One . . . two . . . three . . . four. Hmmm . . . . Bell Avenue—price is fifty dollars. Jamal read the golden letters on the board. I think I'll pass. I'd rather buy a higher priced property."

"Go ahead, Lilly, you go next," said Jimmy. So like Jamal, Lilly rolled the dice on the floor. She moved the pink minivan token six spaces to the space marked Blue Cloud Airlines, price is one hundred dollars. "I'll buy it," she said and handed Jimmy two, fifty-dollar bills. Jimmy looked through the yellow cards and found the card for Blue Cloud Airlines and handed it to Lilly.

"OK, now I'll go," announced Jimmy and rolled the dice. Jimmy rolled a ten. He landed on a box that said, "Pick a red card." He picked up the top card and read it aloud. "Go to Otto's Antiques and pick up your inheritance."

"Otto's Antiques? . . . Pick up your inheritance?" said Jamal, scrunching his eyebrows together and scratching his head. "This is one weird game. Does it say how much you will get?"

"No, and there is no Otto's Antiques on the board," answered Lilly, who was looking over Jimmy's shoulder at the card.

"No, but there is an Otto's Antiques on Oak Street," said Jimmy matter-of-factly.

"Oh yeah. It's right next door to the bike shop," said Lilly.

"That creepy place," said Jamal, shuddering. "It doesn't even look open."

"Keep your tokens and money for now," said Jimmy. Carefully, he put the extra tokens, the cards, and the rest of the money back in the drawer of The Game. Then, he gently put The Game back in the crate and closed the lock with a snap. "Let's go," he said, walking out the door.

"Let's go where?" asked Jamal, hopping on his bike. "I'm not going to any creepy antique store."

"Mom is expecting us at home," said Lilly with authority as she got on her bike.

But they followed Jimmy to Oak Street, anyhow.

Chapter 3

"IT'S A QUARTER to four already," said Jamal, pedaling his chubby legs hard to stay in their little caravan of bikes. "The store is probably closed by now. Anyway, it's two hours until dinner time and I'm starved."

"I'm only going with you because Mom told me to keep an eye on you. We have to go home right after we go to the antique shop," said Lilly, still trying to be in charge. "But if we are late then you get the blame, Jimmy, not me."

Jimmy ignored Jamal and Lilly and kept on going. Ten minutes later, they pulled up to a small storefront. It was made up of a large picture window and a door.

"Otto's Antiques: We Buy and Sell," said Jamal, reading the sign above the door. "Look at the letters on the sign. They are so faded that you can hardly read them. Like I told you—this place is creepy."

Before going in, Jimmy, Jamal, and Lilly looked in the picture window, which was filled with antiques. "Looks like a bunch of dusty old junk to me," said Lilly with disgust.

In the window, among the other items jammed together, were some drinking mugs that looked more like faces with handles on them. Next to the mugs were some blue and white dishes decorated with trees and a bridge. "Look at that great big, gold statue of a woman dressed in a bed sheet that's been wrapped around her. She is holding some kind of pitcher," said Jamal.

"Ugly, if you ask me," said Lilly, fluffing her hair and glaring at her brother.

Jimmy was staring at something on the bottom shelf. "Hmmm?" he said to himself.

"What?" Jamal asked. "What do you see?"

Instead of answering, Jimmy walked to the door and opened it. An old cowbell hanging on the back of the door clanged to announce their arrival.

"This store is gross. It smells old and musty," said Lilly, looking around. "It's just like the front window, completely crammed with junk."

"You mean antiques," corrected Jimmy. "Not junk."

"It's so dim in here," said Jamal nervously. "It makes everything look ever older and creepier."

It wasn't long before they heard a door in the back of the store creak open. Through the door came an old man. He appeared very short as he moved behind a showcase. It wasn't until he turned the corner that they saw he was sitting in a wheelchair.

"Hi, Jimmy," said the man in the wheelchair. His voice was soft and kind. "I've been expecting you."

"Hi, Otto," answered Jimmy like he was talking to a friend on the playground at school. "Can I see the little statue on the bottom shelf in the window? You know . . . the one that kinda looks like you."

"Ah, yes," said Otto with a chuckle. "I've been getting quite a few comments about that statue."

Like the statue, Otto was a small, older man. He had lots of white hair that was combed neatly with a part on one side. His face had a slight roundness to it, with a mustache that curled up a little on each cheek. Otto's bright blue eyes sparkled behind black, round-rimmed glasses. Also like the statue in the window, Otto was wearing a green plaid jacket with a matching green bow tie. Unlike the statue, Otto was not standing up. He was in a wheelchair.

Lilly and Jamal had been silently looking from Jimmy to Otto. Lilly's mouth was open with surprise and confusion.

"I thought seeing the museum token in The Game was the surprise of the day, but I was wrong," said Lilly, shaking her head. "But now that I think of it, why should a boy who plays board games by himself and finds secret compartments with a token that looks exactly like our father's children's museum be a surprise to me at all?" Lilly cracked her gum like a loud exclamation point at the end of her sentence.

"How do you know him?" asked Jamal, looking up from a glass case that was displaying a baseball mitt from 1925.

"I just like to come here now and then to look at all the old stuff." Jimmy answered.

Jimmy pointed at Jamal and Lilly, "This is my elder sister, Lilly. She is three years older than me so my Mom makes her keep an eye on me. And this is Jamal, our good friend, who lives across the street from us."

"Nice to meet any friend or family of Jimmy," said Otto as he wheeled close to the picture window. "Now, Jimmy, reach into the picture window there and get the statue for me."

"I'm supposed to come here and collect my inheritance," Jimmy said as he reached over and grabbed the little man off the shelf. "It says so on the red card from The Game at the museum."

Jimmy reached in and got the small statue. "How much do you want for it?" he asked.

Otto smiled and winked. "Just keep the statue for now. It might come in handy. We'll talk about the money another time."

"What about the inheritance?" Lilly blurted out. "Not that I care," she added quickly. "I just want to take care of everything so we can go home already. I'm in charge of my brother, you know. I've got responsibilities." Lilly blew a small bubble with her gum as she stared at Otto.

Otto chuckled softly. "You should explore downstairs. I think you'll find what you are looking for down there."

"Thanks," said Jimmy. He slipped the statue into his pants' pocket, opened the basement door, and flipped on the light switch.

There was even less light downstairs than in the shop upstairs. Jimmy led the way down the creaking steps.

"It looks scary down here," said Jamal, starting to shake a little. "I knew I didn't want to come here."

"Wow!" said Jimmy. "There is much more old stuff down here than upstairs. The shelves are filled from floor to ceiling!"

"Everything is covered with so much dust," said Lilly. "You can hardly tell what anything is."

"Hey, Lilly . . . Jamal. Come here!" Jimmy called. "You're not going to believe this!"

"Achoo! Achoo! Achoo! We have to get out of here," called Lilly as she made her way to Jimmy. "There is way too much dust . . . achoo!"

When Jamal and Lilly found Jimmy, he was sitting on the floor, reading an old black, leather-bound book that was opened across his lap. They kneeled down, one on each side of him.

"You've got to see this," said Jimmy, flipping through the pages.

"What kind of book is it?" asked Jamal, as he lightly closed the book over Jimmy's hand in order to see the front cover.

Lilly brushed off some of the dust to uncover the title. "The Game: How to Play, How to Win, and How to Keep From Getting Lost," said Lilly, reading the title. "Getting lost where?"

"Gameland, of course," said Jamal, laughing and then nervously popped yet another chocolate mini-bite in his mouth.

"No," said Jimmy. "The book says that the real name for the place is Sweet Abundance. Except the word *Sweet* has been crossed out. That's weird. Wait, it goes on to say that once you have found Sweet Abundance, you need this guide book to help you."

"Jimmy, you do know that there is no such place as Sweet Abundance or even just Abundance," said Lilly sweetly like she talks to the little twin girls down the street when she is babysitting them. "OK, so now, why don't we take the book home and look at it some more there."

Jimmy opened the book to the first page, ignoring his sister. "The title of chapter one is 'How to Start,'" he read aloud. "In order to travel in Abundance, once you have found it, you will need the following essential items—The Game money and your own token that comes in The Game."

"Jimmy," said Lilly, feeling a little quiver. "We've all got our tokens and some of The Game money."

Jamal dug in his pocket and pulled out his little dog token and held it out in his open palm. Lilly took the pink minivan token, covered in cute flowers, and did the same.

"So now what Jimmy?" Lilly asked.

"The book is full of guides and suggestions about visiting different locations in Sweet Abundance, but it doesn't tell us how to get there. It just says, 'Once you have found it.'"

"Hey," said Jamal. "Lilly is right. Let's take the book home and come back tomorrow. This is getting creepier by the minute."

That's when they heard noise coming from behind the back wall of the basement. It sounded like a crowd of people that were pretty excited about something.

Jimmy closed the book and tucked it under his arm. Slowly, silently, they made their way through the tall dusty shelves over to the back wall. They followed the noise to help guide them.

They got to the back wall. "There's nothing here but shelves full of super dusty old junk . . . I mean . . . antiques," said Lilly. "Achoo!"

"Look!" said Jimmy excitedly. "Over there in the corner. The shelves don't go all the way to the ceiling. There is a dusty, old, dark gray curtain covered in strange curlicue designs, hanging on the wall above the shelves."

Jimmy walked over to the curtain and lifted the corner. Then, because of a bright light that shown out, he quickly put the corner of the curtain back down.

"Whoa!" said Lilly. "Now that is one mega-bright light."

Jimmy turned and ran to the other side of the basement.

"Where are you going, Jimmy?" Jamal called to him. "Don't leave me down here!"

"I'm getting a stepladder," Jimmy answered. "I'm sure I saw one near the foot of the stairs. Oh, here it is. Jamal, help me carry it over to the curtain."

"This is a mistake," said Jamal, as he and Jimmy lugged the small stepladder over to the curtain.

Jimmy opened the ladder and climbed two steps and put his hand over his eyes like a little visor.

"It's too bright," said Jamal. "You'll go blind if you look in there. It's just like looking at the sun. C'mon, Jimmy, let's get out of here before it's too late!"

"No," answered Jimmy. "It's just that it's so dim down here our eyes aren't used to it." Then he ducked under the curtain. All Lilly and Jamal could see were his legs on the stepladder, illuminated by a bright light.

Jamal and Lilly quickly put their hands above their eyes to protect themselves from the bright light.

Then they heard Jimmy pull the window up. "Wow! This is so cool!"

Lilly and Jamal watched Jimmy's legs disappear, as he climbed the rest of the way through the window.

Chapter 4

"YOU GUYS SHOULD see this," said Jimmy from the other side of the curtain.

There was a loud creak as Jimmy pulled the curtains open. He was smiling at them from the other side of the window. Lilly and Jamal stepped back and gasped when they saw Jimmy. The gum fell out of Lilly's mouth, landed on her shoe, and bounced off but she didn't even notice. Jamal's eyes were wide open, and when he tried to speak all that came out was, "Ah . . . ah . . . ah."

Lilly blinked her eyes to make sure she was seeing right. "Am I dreaming?" she said, putting her hands up to her mouth.

"This is awesome," said Jimmy, looking down at himself. "I've turned into a cartoon. Come on over. It doesn't hurt or anything."

Jimmy stuck his hand back through the window to help them through. Lilly gave a little shriek as Jimmy's hand turned back into a non-cartoon hand when it crossed into the basement. Lilly reached out with her hand and Jimmy began pulling her through the window.

"Hey, it really doesn't hurt, it just tickles a little," said Lilly, giggling. "Look at me! I'm a cartoon!"

"Pull me through too!" said Jamal, reaching his hand through the window. "I'm not staying here."

"You were right, Jimmy. This is cool," said Jamal after they pulled him through. "And I'm used to the light already. The light is just like a bright summer day."

"Maybe I'm dreaming, and any minute I'm going to wake up," said Lilly. "But if I'm not dreaming then where are we?"

"Well, obviously, we are in a cartoon world," said Jimmy, looking around at all the cartoon houses, stores, cars, and trees. It looks like Sweet Abundance is real after all.

"Did you notice that the colors of everything here are like in a comic book?" said Jamal, looking around. "It's what our art teacher calls primary colors. Everything here is, pretty much, just one of the basic colors from your smallest crayon box—red, blue, green, and yellow."

"Look," said Lilly. "The people here look like us. Our hair looks like molded clay, and our shoes are big and round."

"The buildings are kind of funny looking," added Jamal. "Their walls aren't straight up and down like normal buildings. Instead they are bulgy and round. Hey, did you see that? One of the buildings moved a little."

"Check out the cars," said Jimmy, pointing at the street.

Cars were moving quickly up and down the street. They didn't move exactly like real cars do. One car was going so fast around the corner that it stretched around to make the curve. The back of the car snapped back behind the front like a rubber band. The headlights were like eyes. They looked from side to side before crossing an intersection. The grills in the front of the cars turned into smiles or frowns.

"Listen to that crowd of people over there," said Jamal. "That was the noise we heard in the basement of Otto's store."

Jimmy, Lilly and Jamal started walking over to a group of people gathered near a small, red brick building. People leaned toward each other, each one talking excitedly. "I wish I could see what is going on in that building," said Jimmy.

Jamal bent over and made a little step with his hands by lacing his fingers together in front of his round belly. Jimmy raised his foot and put it in Jamal's hands. Then he pushed himself up with his other foot and balanced himself by putting his hands on Jamal's shoulders.

"Hey, now I can see over the crowd. The sign on the building says, 'Dead End,'" said Jimmy jumping back down.

"Somebody's going to Dead End!" said Jamal, sounding a little scared.

"Who is it?" Lilly asked. "And what is Dead End?"

"You don't know dear?" said a cartoon woman from the crowd.

"No," they all said together.

"It's Mr. Isadore Benefactor! It's so shocking for him to be in Dead End!" cried the cartoon woman. "If you land in Dead End then you are stuck there until someone gets you out."

"We don't know him," answered Jimmy.

The woman's mouth opened in a perfect "o." Her eyes opened and bulged out like two Ping-Pong balls on springs. Her red hat, with a blue brim that folded up over her forehead, flew up a foot in the air.

"Pull yourself together," said Jimmy calmly. "We're new around here."

And that is exactly what she did. In a flash, she was back to normal. Well, as normal as a cartoon woman can be.

"Who is Mr. Isadore Benefactor?" Jamal asked from behind Lilly's back, where he was hiding like a "scaredy" cat.

"Why, he is the Mayor of Sweet Abundance and President of the Pot's in the Middle Bank," the cartoon woman explained.

Jamal looked at Jimmy. "Pot's in the Middle?"

"Think Jamal," said Jimmy. "When we play board games where do we put the 'pot' of money?"

"Oh yeah," said Jamal, smiling, getting the idea. Then his face got confused again. "But the 'pot' goes in the middle of the game board. Where do the people here keep their money?"

The cartoon woman looked kindly at them. "Why, our bank stands in the middle of the square. It's all right there in your guide book," she said, pointing her white-gloved finger to the book tucked under Jimmy's arm.

Jimmy opened the book and flipped over to the index to look up "banks." "Here it is. The First National Pot's in the Middle Bank Page thirty-six. Hmmm . . . let's see . . . it says the bank has been in the middle of the Square pretty much since the beginning. And then, it simply says, 'Your money is safe with us.'"

"You can see the bank from anywhere in Sweet Abundance," said a cartoon man from the crowd. He pointed up and Lilly, Jamal, and Jimmy all turned their heads up to see a huge, dark, towering building. It was bigger than any building they'd seen in Sweet Abundance so far.

Suddenly, a funny, little blue van pulled up to the curb with a screech. The van looked excited. The headlights moved quickly back and forth and the grill was smiling. Sitting on top of the van was a big model of a TV camera that bobbed around with every move that the van made. On one side of the van was a sign that read,

<blockquote>
Abundance TV 7

We Bring You News from

Every Square of Sweet Abundance!
</blockquote>

A woman and a cameraman hopped out of the van and walked quickly toward the crowd. The cameraman carried a TV camera on his shoulder and the woman had a pad of paper and pencil in her hands. They both had "Press" ID cards hanging around their necks.

The crowd parted for them to get through to the Dead End building. Lilly, Jamal, and Jimmy looked at the man who was looking out the only window in the small brick building.

"What's Otto doing in Dead End?" asked Jamal. "How did he get here?"

"That's not Otto," said Lilly. "Don't you remember? Otto has white hair. That guy has black hair."

They walked close to the window. "Isadore, is that you?" asked Jimmy.

"Yes, sadly, it's me, boy. I was hoping you would be along." Isadore nervously straightened his green bow tie that matched his green plaid jacket.

"You know him?" said Jamal and Lilly in total disbelief.

"How'd you get stuck in Dead End?" asked Jimmy.

"It's that rogue, John Heartless," said Isadore sadly. "He tricked me so I'd land in Dead End. I know that it's just part of his evil plan to take over Sweet Abundance. Ah, it's a sad day since he's been around."

"Is that why the word *Sweet* was crossed off in the guide book?" asked Jimmy.

"Yes," he is already making changes around here.

"But why would you create such a guy?" asked Jimmy.

"Create him?" Lilly practically screamed. "OK, Jimmy, you had better tell us what's going on around here."

"It's a long story, young lady," said Isadore. "And if I don't get out soon it will have a terrible end."

"How can we help?" asked Jimmy.

Mr. Benefactor (Isadore) waved to Jimmy to come close to the window. Jimmy walked close to the window and leaned in as close as he could. Then Isadore whispered something to him.

"OK, kids, Outta the way! We have an interview to do," shouted the man with the camera on his shoulder.

"We'll be back soon," Jimmy called to Isadore. "Don't worry,"

"Now, Mr. Benefactor," said the tall woman reporter with long wavy black hair and a short red dress. She had her pencil and pad ready to take notes. "I've got a few questions for you."

Lilly and Jamal didn't get to hear her questions because Jimmy was walking away so fast. They had to practically run to keep up with him.

They crossed the street to a little city park where Jimmy plopped himself down right in the middle of a long bench. He opened the guide book and started flipping through the pages. Lilly sat down on one side of Jimmy and Jamal sat down on the other.

"Hmmm . . . traveling tips . . . I bet this could be the section to help us," said Jimmy.

"How do you know Isadore?" Lilly asked quietly, interrupting Jimmy.

"Are we going to try and get him out of Dead End?" added Jamal.

Jimmy looked up from the guide book. "OK, I guess it's time I answered your questions. First, I know Isadore because I met him once at Otto's store. He is Otto's younger brother, and he is a cartoonist. Second, yes we are going to get him out of Dead End. And third, before you ask, Isadore told me how to get him out which I will explain later."

Jamal and Lilly just looked at each other.

"It says here," said Jimmy, looking back in the guide book and running his finger across the page. "Your tokens may be brought to life size. All you need to do is add water . . . Lilly you have your little van token in your pocket, don't you?"

"Yes, but what do they mean just add water?" she asked as she pulled the little van token out of her pocket.

"I don't know, but for now, just put it on the ground," said Jimmy.

Lilly put it on the ground and the three of them waited to watch it grow to life size. But it didn't. The little van token just sat there doing nothing.

"Jimmy, the book says to add water," Lilly reminded him.

"Let's see," said Jimmy, looking around. "Where is a good place to get some water?"

Jamal didn't say a word. He just bent over and spit right smack on the little van token. Jamal looked at Jimmy's and Lilly's shocked faces. "What? It's wet, isn't it?"

And then, without warning, Jamal took out his little wiener dog token, spat on it, and put it on the ground next to the little van.

"Jamal! What'd you do that for?" cried Lilly. "What are we going to do with a dog?"

"I don't know," said Jamal, shrugging his shoulders. "We did it to your token so I thought I'd do it to mine. Anyway, I've always wanted a dog, but my parents have terrible allergies so I can't have one."

Again, they waited. They sat there looking at the van and the dog token, not knowing what was going to happen. It wasn't long before they heard a crackling sound. Sort of like someone unwrapping a package covered with plastic wrap.

Then the popping sound started. "Cool!" said Jamal. "It sounds like someone's making popcorn."

With little jerks and hops, the van began to grow. They couldn't see the dog token anymore. It was lost under the van.

Finally, after several minutes, a small pink minivan with large flowers decorating the sides stood in front of them. They looked under the van but saw no dog. "I guess my token is a 'dud,'" said Jamal sadly.

The van's front seat was made for two, but Jimmy, Lilly, and Jamal hopped in and fit just fine.

Chapter 5

JIMMY, SITTING BEHIND the wheel, opened the guide book to the middle. The book lay open across his legs. It was a map of Sweet Abundance. Sadly, the word "Sweet" was crossed out.

"Where to?" asked Jamal as he moved the open book onto his lap.

"First stop, The Welcome Center," answered Jimmy, leaning over from behind the wheel and running his finger over the map to find the "Welcome Center." "Then we will be off to Make Your Fortune."

"OK," said Jamal, studying the map. "From Dead End we have to go down Schoolhouse Street, past the Sweet Abundance Food Market, then down Vienna Avenue. After that we pass the Blue Cloud Airlines and finally down Philadelphia Avenue. The Welcome Center is on the next block."

"All the streets are one way streets," said Lilly, looking over the map. "How weird is that? You can only go forward. You can't turn around. The streets of Sweet Abundance are set up like a game board. And all the streets make a path around the big Square where Pot's in the Middle Bank stands."

Just as Jimmy reached to push the blue button on the dashboard that was marked "start," they heard some barking underneath the van; then a scurrying, scratching noise. Suddenly, a cute little dachshund (wiener dog) ran out from under the van and began running wildly around the park.

"Wow! Look at him go!" said Jamal. The dog zoomed twice around a tree and then ran under a park bench where it sat down, staring right at the van.

"Here, boy!" shouted Jamal and opened the van door. In a flash, the dog jumped in, right onto Jamal's lap. He began immediately licking the chocolate off Jamal's cheek. "See, he likes me," said Jamal, smiling and scratching the dog under its long snout. "What's your name, boy?"

"How am I supposed to know? I'm just a token," answered the dog in perfectly clear words.

They all turned surprised faces to each other. Jamal started laughing. "He talks!"

"Of course, I talk," replied the dog. "All dogs talk. It's just that people never really stop to listen."

"OK, I'm definitely sound asleep in my bed at home having a weird dream," said Lilly. "Maybe it was the hot dog that I ate for lunch."

"What should we call you?" asked Jamal.

"Jamal, you do realize that you are talking to a dog," said Lilly, shaking her head, with her eyes open wide. "Jimmy, c'mon, you don't think this is strange?"

"Lilly, we are cartoon people in a cartoon world. Why should a talking dog shock you?" Jimmy answered calmly.

"You're right. You're right, Jimmy," said Lilly, biting lightly on her pearl-pink polished nail. "But when I wake up from this dream, my friends will never believe me."

"Ah-hem," said the small dachshund, clearing its throat. "You asked about a name for me. Let me think. Well . . . I guess you could call me Bernard. I always wished they had made me a St. Bernard. You know, because they get to rescue people . . . get their picture in the newspaper . . . become a hero. Now that would be a great job for a dog!"

"OK then, Bernard it will be," said Jimmy as he pushed the blue button on the dashboard marked "start." He put his foot on the gas pedal, and the van was off, zipping down the street.

"Let . . . the sun shine," sang a voice coming from a speaker where the radio would normally be. "Let . . . the sun shine in. La . . . la . . . la . . . la. I can never remember the rest of the words to that song."

Jamal started to laugh again. "Of course, it's a singing van, what else?" Then shaking nervously, he unwrapped another mini-bite candy and popped it in his mouth.

"Yum . . . chocolate. Can I have some?" asked the voice from the speaker. Jamal just stared silently at the speaker.

Jimmy patted the dashboard. "Not now. Let's wait until we get finished at the Welcome Center."

They drove down Schoolhouse Street to Virginia Avenue. Soon they passed the Sweet Abundance Food Market and then down Vienna Road. At the end of the street, there stood a most unusual building.

At first glance, looking out the van window, it looked like an ordinary two-story brick building. There were two windows on the second floor, except that these windows had shades that fluttered like eyelashes.

"Why in the world is there a long pipe sticking out of the two sides of that building?" asked Jamal.

"Wait, look at the open hands on the end of the two pipes," called Lilly.

"It looks like the building is welcoming us with open arms!" said Jimmy. "That is definitely cool."

"All welcome. Especially Visitors," Lilly read the sign above the door. "This should be good."

"You stay in the car, Bernard," said Jamal.

"Sure. Anything you say, Jamal. You're the master. I'm the dog. I'll just curl up on the back seat and wait. No problem."

Jimmy, Lilly, and Jamal walked up the sidewalk toward the Welcome Center Building. They turned around when they heard the click of Bernard's paws following right behind.

"What?" Bernard asked. He tilted his head to the side to look as cute and innocent as possible.

"Bernard. You were supposed to stay!" scolded Jamal.

"Well . . . I meant to . . . really I did. It's just that I hate to be left alone."

Jamal looked at Lilly and Jimmy and shrugged his shoulders. "I kinda get how he feels."

Lilly laughed. "You two make a great pair."

Jimmy, Lilly, Jamal, and now Bernard walked through the door right into a large open room. "This room reminds me of the little motel we stayed at last summer on our way to see Granny and Gramps in Colorado," said Lilly.

"Look, there is a counter where you sign in, and over there is a display rack of pamphlets telling visitors where to visit. Here is one that says, don't leave without a visit to Make Your Fortune," said Jimmy.

It was then that Jimmy looked up and noticed two large pictures hanging on the wall behind the counter.

"This is not good," said Jimmy, pointing to the pictures.

"Hey, that one is a picture of Isadore," said Lilly.

The other was a picture of a sinister-looking man. His eyes were dark, and he had a mustache and a goatee. He was dressed all in black except for a king's crown on his head.

"I bet that's John Heartless!" said Jamal. "What's with the crown?"

"Wearing the crown is part of his takeover," said Jimmy with a scowl. "He thinks he is going to be king of Sweet Abundance."

Jimmy quickly opened the guide book and began flipping through the pages and running his finger under words on a page.

Lilly walked over to the counter and tapped the silver bell. She looked over her shoulder. "I better handle this," she said in her best in-charge voice.

A young girl came out wearing a shirt and a ball cap; both with "Welcome to Sweet Abundance" stitched on them with an X over the word Sweet. "Good afternoon," she said smiling. "Are you visitors?"

"Yes," said Jimmy. "The guide book says that you need to get your visitor pack at the Welcome Center, and the three of us are visitors."

The girl reached under the counter and took out a large blue book with the word "Visitors" printed in fancy letters on the cover. "Please step forward and sign our guest register."

As everyone, except Bernard, stepped forward the girl pulled out a large sign that said, "Visitors Are Allowed to Stay Only for Three Days."

"What is that all about?" asked Lilly. Her eyebrows were crunched together.

"Oh, it is a new rule that was just made by Mr. Heartless. He is making the decisions now," answered Welcoming Girl. She opened the "visitors" book to the next available page. "I'll be right back," she said as she went out of the room.

They all came forward and signed their names in the book. "What in the world!" Lilly gasped. "Look! Our signatures are changing."

"Now our names are completely gone!" cried Jamal. "All that is left is three straight lines."

"Wait a minute," said Jimmy with a big smile. "The lines are starting to move around the page. This is definitely amazing."

Like three snakes, the three lines slithered around the page. They made strange figures, and then, finally, each line twisted around into a simple line drawing. There, in the middle of the page, were three pictures. There was one picture of Lilly, one of Jamal and one of Jimmy.

"Cool!" said all three together.

In a short time Welcoming Girl returned carrying three drawstring bags. "Inside each bag," explained the girl, "is your visitor's pass, two hundred in The Game money, a coupon to select two red cards—one from the Welcome Center and one from Make Your Fortune. These items, of course are only good for the three days you are allowed to stay."

"What happens if we stay longer?" asked Jamal.

"Why, you land in Dead End," she said seriously. "There is only one way to get out of Dead End. Someone picks a red card that says, Dead End Rescue Card and brings it to you. Then you are free to leave Dead End.

"We've definitely got to get Isadore out of Dead End," said Jimmy as he took his visitor's bag from Welcoming Girl.

"Would you like to pick your red cards now?" asked the girl.

"Yeah, sure," Jimmy said easily, and they all walked up to the locked box on the counter that was marked Red Cards.

Lilly stepped forward as Welcoming Girl unlocked the box. "Close your eyes, please," she instructed. "Then reach in and take the top card."

Lilly closed her eyes, reached in and took the top card. "You win the price of an airline ticket from Blue Cloud Airlines," she read. "Collect two hundred dollars."

"Cash it in here," said Welcoming Girl taking the card from Lilly. She took two hundred dollars in The Game money from the cash drawer, which was under the counter, and then handed it to Lilly. The money went right into Lilly's pocket.

Jamal went next. He closed his eyes and picked the next card and then read it to himself. "Oh no," he moaned.

"That bad?" said Lilly, chewing a new piece of gum and nervously fluffing her red curls with her fingers.

"You have won fifty dollars in the Annual Sweet Abundance Beauty Contest," Jamal read slowly and very softly—so that no one would notice what he had read.

Lilly put her hand to her mouth to keep in the giggle. Jimmy looked away trying not to let his smile turn into a full-blown laugh.

"Well, I don't think it's so funny," Jamal complained as Welcoming Girl placed a large red ribbon across his pudgy belly.

"Congratulations," said Lilly snorting and laughing at the same time.

Bernard started rolling over on this back, chuckling. "Yeah . . . congratulations, Jamal."

Jimmy shook his head smiling broadly. "OK, Jamal you can take the ribbon off."

"I'll cash that for you," said Welcoming Girl without even a hint of a smile. She took back the ribbon and the red card. "She then handed Jamal fifty dollars in The Game money."

Jimmy stepped forward, closed his eyes, as if making a wish, and picked his card. "Because of your efforts to be more 'green', you collect two hundred dollars from the Sweet Abundance Food Market," he read aloud. "Rats, that wasn't the one I wanted."

Jimmy turned in the card for the two hundred dollars.

They all walked back to the car in silence; the only sound was the click click of Bernard's paws on the ground. Jimmy pushed the blue start button in the car. "Next stop . . . Make Your Fortune."

"Oh what a beautiful morning," sang the little car as it began to move down the street. "Oh what a beautiful day . . . I've got a beautiful feeling . . . That . . . everything's going my way."

"Were you hoping to pick the Dead End Rescue Card?" asked Lilly.

"Yep," said Jimmy.

"Is that what Isadore told you to do to get him out of Dead End?" asked Lilly.

"Yes, but I'm not giving up," said Jimmy, smiling at Lilly and Jamal like he did when he was playing one of his board games. "There is always more than one strategy to win a game."

"Speaking of not giving up . . . how about some of that chocolate?" said the voice coming from the speaker.

Jamal dug in his pocket to get out a mini-bite candy and took off the wrapper. "Where should I put it?"

"Open the glove compartment, and toss it in," said a voice coming from the speaker.

Jamal opened the glove compartment door. Inside the door was a sign that said, "Fuel—something yummy I hope."

Jamal tossed the mini-bite into the glove compartment and quickly closed the door. As they drove along, they heard soft little munching sounds with an occasional "yum . . . delicious." And finally, "Thank you very much."

"What's your name?" asked Jimmy as if he was making a new friend.

"Well . . . actually . . . just like Bernard I never got a name," said the voice from the speaker. "They don't name tokens you know. But I'm awfully fond of the name Randy. You see, Randy can either be a girl or boy's name—and since I'm neither, Randy fits just fine."

"Then Randy it is!" said Jimmy, smiling down at the speaker.

It was then that they pulled up to another unusual building. It looked like something you would see in Las Vegas on their gambling strip. The building was covered with signs that were flashing and blinking. Some signs were even turning around. One sign said, "Win Big Money."

There was another sign made up of several horses whose legs moved back and forth as if they were racing. "Look at the horse racing sign," said Jamal. "This place is obviously all about gambling and making money."

The biggest sign said, "This is where you can *make your fortune.*"

"Welcome to Make Your Fortune and another try at the red cards," said Lilly, actually smiling at Jimmy and Jamal. "I hope one of us picks the Dead End Rescue Card so Isadore can get out of Dead End."

"Me too," answered Jimmy, smiling back at his sister.

"Good luck when you go in there," said Randy, giggling. "Get it? You know. Good luck . . . Gambling."

"Real funny. A car with a sense of humor," said Jamal, shaking his head and rolling his eyes.

Jimmy, Jamal, Lilly, and Bernard headed toward the front door. But before they reached the door, it began to open by itself with the sound of a loud horn playing the melody to announce a horse race.

Jamal started to shake. "I've got a bad feeling about this place. I really don't think we should go in there."

Suddenly, a tall man dressed all in black opened the door the rest of the way. The man had on a long black coat with a king's crown on his head. His face was the same face as in the picture behind the counter at the Welcome Center.

"Come in Jimmy, Lilly, and Jamal," he said in a deep, gravelly voice. "And let's not forget your little dog too." He stretched out his arm and guided the three children and Bernard into the Make Your Fortune building.

"How do you know our names?" asked Jimmy as he walked through the door.

"Why, my child, you just came from the Welcome Center where you got your visitor's passes. I recognized you from your pictures. You see, I will soon be the king of Abundance, and therefore, it is my job to know everyone who is here, even if they're here for a visit."

"Time for Bernard and I to go," said Jamal in a voice that he tried to make cheery. "Bernard and I will wait for you guys with Randy."

"Not before you've spent some time at Make Your Fortune," said the tall man in the dark coat. The door closed with a loud bang, and Jamal jumped and began to shake again.

"Let me introduce myself. I am the great and very powerful John Heartless . . . soon to be the king of Abundance."

"I guess that explains the crown," said Jimmy.

"I thought it was a nice touch," said John Heartless, patting the crown on his head.

Jamal and Lilly looked silently at each other but did not speak.

Unlike the bright quiet room at the Welcome Center, Make Your Fortune was dark and very noisy. "Bingo!" shouted a cartoon man from a corner where they were playing Bingo. Just like the lady near the Dead End, his green hat shot up a foot in the air and his eyes bugged out like two Ping-Pong balls on springs.

In another corner was a group sitting around a table. They were playing cards. Coins and dollars were being thrown to the middle of the table.

"Looks like everybody is trying to win money," said Lilly.

"Then Make Your Fortune is a good name for the place," answered Jimmy.

"Which game do you want to play?" asked John Heartless, leaning right into Jimmy's face.

"No game," said Jimmy flatly. "We just came to pick our red cards. We're visitors and are allowed a free pick."

Little clouds of steam puffed out of John Heartless's ears. The white part of his eyes turned red. "That's true. You are allowed a free pick," he said in a quiet but definitely angry voice. "But that will all change—soon!"

Bernard growled and started barking at John Heartless's feet. Long bony fingers reached down and scooped up the little dachshund. John Heartless glared into the dog's eyes and sneered. "Quiet, you little mutt, or I'll make dog food out of you!"

Bernard squirmed out of his grasp and ran like a shot behind Jamal's legs.

At the back of the large room, John Heartless opened a door marked, Office. "The red cards are in here," he growled.

"He looks real mad," said Jamal softly to Jimmy and Lilly as they walked toward the office door. Bernard followed behind; his nails clicked on the hard floor. "I knew coming in here was a bad idea."

Inside the office, on a desk was the same kind of box they saw at the Welcome Center. John Heartless unlocked the box. "Go ahead, Jimmy, pick," he sneered.

Jimmy stepped up to the box, glancing nervously at the tall man in the dark suit, and cape. He pulled out a red card. "Pay one hundred dollars on unpaid taxes," he read, sadly shaking his head.

John Heartless stuck out his hand. "Pay up now!" he practically shouted.

Jimmy pulled out some of The Game money from in his pocket and handed John Heartless two fifty-dollar bills.

John Heartless was smiling now and twirling the end of his mustache with his fingers. "You were lucky. The other cards are much worse." He threw his head back and let out a loud, sinister laugh. "Now, how about you, Jamal?"

"Me?" answered Jamal, shaking like it was ten degrees. He stuck his hand in his pocket to take out a mini-bite when John Heartless leaned into his face, "Yes, you! You little . . ."

Brave Bernard saw Jamal shaking with fright and started barking and running around John Heartless's feet. John Heartless bent down to make a grab for Bernard but then his crown fell off his head and rolled toward the back of the room. As John Heartless chased after his crown, Bernard began to race for the door.

"I'm out of here, too," said Jamal and began to run. Jimmy and Lilly were right behind.

Jimmy pulled the door open as the horns once again announced a race. But this time they stepped out into the bright daylight—out to freedom.

Before they had taken two steps down the front path to where Randy waited for them, John Heartless stuck his head out the door. He stretched his neck, like a big spring so that he was eyeball-to-eyeball with Jimmy. "Just for your information, young man, there are no Dead End Rescue Cards in the pile. There are no Dead End Rescue Cards anywhere in Abundance for that matter. I took care of that. Heh . . . heh . . . heh!" He laughed his evil laugh as his head returned to its normal place.

Randy was waiting with the engine running as Jimmy, Lilly, Jamal, and Bernard piled in and closed Randy's door. Soon they were driving on Indiana Avenue.

"So John Heartless got rid of all the Dead End Rescue Cards," said Jamal in a quiet voice. "Now what are we going to do?"

"It just means that we have to go with Isadore's backup plan," said Jimmy. "I really hoped we wouldn't have to do it . . . but . . ."

"But what?" Lilly, Jamal, Randy, and Bernard all asked together.

"It's the only way to get Isadore out of Dead End," Jimmy answered. "It's the only way to save the people of Sweet Abundance from John Heartless. And it's the only way for us to get back home."

"Boy, oh boy, I hate when these kinds of things happen," said Jamal sadly. "Now we'll never get out of here. What will my Mom and Dad think? They will have lost their little Jamal. Their only child lost forever and . . ."

"Jamal! Cool it!" cried Jimmy, "We'll get out of here . . . you'll see."

Chapter 6

THEY DROVE IN silence. Jimmy looked at the map. "We're now headed toward Philadelphia Avenue," Jimmy reported.

They passed the Blue Cloud Airlines station. "Look at the big model of an airplane up there on the roof of the station building," said Lilly, smiling. "I've got to admit, that was pretty clever."

"We are getting close to another Make Your Fortune building," announced Randy. "There are two in Sweet Abundance you know. The second one was just added. You can guess whose idea that was."

"Look, it is identical to the other Make Your Fortune building. Do you think John Heartless is in there?" asked Lilly.

"I can almost feel him watching us," said Jamal, shuddering.

"Hey, I don't want to see him again if I can help it," said Jimmy. "Let's go right past."

"Don't blame you a bit," said Randy. And with that, the little van hurried past the second Make Your Fortune building as fast as it could go.

They entered Philadelphia Avenue onto a street lined with very old but very beautiful homes and hotels. All the buildings were made of wood with lots of lacy filigree decorating the doors and windows.

"All the houses have large porches decorated with lots of beautiful flowers and comfy rocking chairs," said Lilly. "I wish we had a house with a big porch like that."

"Hey, look," said Jamal, pointing to one porch with a group of people sitting around a table laughing together as they shared a meal. "They look like they are having fun."

"Pit stop," yelled Bernard. "Let me out. I'll be quick about it."

They all got out to "stretch their legs" while Bernard ran behind a big tree. They began strolling down the shady sidewalk enjoying the sunny day and the beautiful homes. "Hey, wait for me!" called Bernard as he ran to join them. They walked a little farther down the street when Jimmy noticed a mailbox with the name I. M. Benefactor on it.

"This must be where Isadore lives!" said Jimmy. "It's just like all the other houses with a porch and flowers, but look, this house has special green and white striped awnings over the windows. Do you notice something in the middle stripe?"

"Oh yeah," said Jamal. "There is a big dollar sign in the middle white stripe."

"Well, it certainly makes sense. He is the president of the bank after all," said Lilly with her elder sister authority. "But wait! Look at the red sign on the front door."

Jimmy read, "Keep out! Future home of John Heartless."

"Let's go!" said Jimmy. "Isadore is in real trouble."

They all ran back to the van. "Hurry up! We've got no time to waste!" said a very serious voice from the speaker. Randy was off like a shot but there was no singing this time. That should have been a warning for our travelers of what was to come.

Chapter 7

AFTER PASSING THE last house on Philadelphia Avenue, they almost immediately had to slow down. There was another big sign at the side of the road that said, "Slow down! You have reached Pot's in the Middle Bank. Please enter the appropriate booth."

It was like getting on to the turnpike. There were two booths to choose from. One was marked: Those going to Pot's in the Middle Bank, stop here. The other booth was marked: Those not stopping at Pot's in the Middle Bank, pass through.

"Which booth do you want to go to?" Randy asked. "Do you want to pass through?"

"No," said Jimmy. We're going to Pot's in the Middle Bank.

"We are?" Jamal and Lilly asked together.

"Yep," Jimmy answered. "It's part of Isadore's backup plan."

"OMG, Jimmy. Now I've really had it!" Lilly said. Her face was turning as red as her red curls. "Mom left me in charge of watching you, and yet, I do not know what is happening here. We are not moving one inch until you explain what exactly is going on."

"She's right, Jimmy," said Bernard. "We all would like to know."

"OK, then, let's pull into this rest stop area before going to the booth," said Jimmy. "We can have a snack, and I'll tell you a little more of what I know."

Even before Jimmy had a chance to turn the wheel, the little van turned into the rest area. Jamal immediately jumped out of the van and made a dash for the rest area building. "Bernard is not the only one who needs a tree," he called out, running as fast as he could.

Soon they were all sitting on the grass near Randy, eating snacks from the vending machines. All eyes were on Jimmy waiting for him to start explaining.

"C'mon, Jimmy," said Jamal, who was stuffing potato chips in his mouth. "I thought we were in a hurry!"

Jimmy was chewing on a pretzel, staring off into space, deep in his own thoughts. "Yes, you are right," answered Jimmy. "I guess I need to tell you the rest of the story."

"Let's see," Jimmy began. "Otto's brother Isadore worked in California as a cartoonist."

"You told us that part already," Lilly reminded him.

"Right . . . OK . . . Isadore was so good at drawing cartoons that he was given more work than he could handle," said Jimmy, calmly continuing his story. "He felt so unhappy with all the stresses and strains in his life. Isadore saw people he loved getting sick or hurt, some losing their jobs. Even his brother Otto got sick and now must spend the rest of his life in a wheelchair."

"So what does all that have to do with Sweet Abundance?" Jamal asked, chewing happily.

"Life is simpler in the cartoons he helped to make. Nobody in cartoons really get sick or hurt. Nobody is hungry or poor. I guess, you could say, they just were. So one day he went to his cabin in the mountains for a weekend retreat. To relax he began drawing pictures of his own little world. He drew his world based on his favorite board game . . ."

"The Game," said Jamal and Lilly, finishing Jimmy's sentence.

"Yes," said Jimmy. "Isadore drew and drew and drew. The weekend came and went. Weeks went by, and he stayed in his cabin in the mountains. He drew so many pictures that soon he believed with all his heart that his world of Sweet Abundance was real. Now, anybody will tell you that if you believe in something strong enough that it will come true. And as you can see, it did."

"This is so cool," said Bernard running around in a circle. "This is about Randy and me."

"OK . . . so where does John Heartless come in?" Lilly asked. "Why would Isadore make an evil guy like him part of Sweet Abundance?"

"Actually, John Heartless was the first visitor from the outside world. He was Isadore's mean boss from California, and Isadore hated him. John Heartless was a mean, dishonest guy, who would stop at nothing to get what he wanted."

"Just like he is now," said Jamal, nervously looking around.

"How'd he get to Sweet Abundance?" asked Lilly.

"John Heartless had come to the cabin looking for Isadore. There was a project to finish, and he wanted Isadore to come back and finish it. He got into Sweet Abundance through a trap door in the floor of the cabin," answered Jimmy. "When he opened the door there it was—Sweet Abundance. Just like when we found it."

Jimmy looked off into space for second. "Everything would have been all right if that evil John Heartless had not gotten his hands on one of Isadore's pens."

"What about Isadore's pens?" Lilly asked.

"It's what Isadore uses to draw everything in Sweet Abundance," answered Jimmy. "Isadore said that he found them in the cabin up in the mountains. He couldn't remember buying them, but he said that he just liked the way they put the ink on the paper."

"How do you know all this?" asked Jamal, scratching Bernard's back.

"Otto told me all about his brother Isadore when I visited his store," Jimmy answered. "I thought he was just making up a great story. I never imagined that it was true. Not until I got here. Then when I saw Isadore, he told me the rest."

Jimmy looked around nervously. "You never know where John Heartless is or where he will show up. So I'll finish telling you what I know so we can get going."

"Now Isadore's pens were kept in the bank somewhere. Somehow, that evil John Heartless stole one of them. Soon the pen will run out of ink and so will John Heartless's power to create. All I can say is that if he ever finds the rest of the pens, we have real trouble."

"How can we help?" asked Lilly, looking seriously at Jimmy, not tossing her curls or checking her nails. "Did Isadore tell you where the rest of the pens are hidden?"

"No, but he gave me a hint," answered Jimmy. "He said that he put the pens in the last place a man like John Heartless would ever set foot."

"And where would that be?" asked Bernard, trotting over to Jimmy.

"I don't know," said Jimmy pulling Bernard up on his lap. "It's our job to figure it out."

"Once we find the pens—if we ever do. What would we do with them?" asked Jamal.

"Oh, that is quite simple," said Jimmy, standing up and throwing his wrappers in the trashcan. "All we have to do is get the pens to Isadore. He can take it from there."

"Hurry up, you guys!" called Randy. "That miserable John Heartless can't be far."

In no time, they were in front of the booth that said: Pot's in the Middle. Stop here.

"What's your business here, young man?" asked the man in the booth.

Jimmy pulled out a "You inherit one hundred dollars" card from his pocket. "I'm going to turn this in at the bank," said Jimmy easily, showing the card to the man in the booth.

"You're a visitor?" asked the man, looking in the van. "What about the rest of them?"

They each took out their visitor's pass and handed it to Jimmy. Then Jimmy handed them to the man in the booth. "Hmmm . . . OK," the man said. "What about the dog?"

"He's a token," volunteered Jamal.

"Oh, so you liquefied him . . . eh . . . well, then, I guess everything is OK," the man said, giving back the cards. "But you must leave as soon as you get your money. No hanging around the bank. New rule, you know. It was passed by Mr. John Heartless himself."

"Where did you get that inherit one-hundred-dollar card?" asked Lilly as they pulled away from the booth.

"Isadore slipped it to me through the window at the Dead End," said Jimmy, putting the card back in his pocket. "He said it might come in handy."

"How would he know that, I wonder?" Lilly asked, not really expecting an answer.

They started driving down a winding, tree-lined path toward Pot's in the Middle Bank. Unlike the trees all over Sweet Abundance that were covered with beautiful, shiny green leaves, these trees, on the path to the bank, were bare of leaves.

"What is with these trees?" asked Lilly. "It looks like winter here."

"Whoa! Look at that black cloud in the sky," added Jamal. "It is casting a dark shadow over the bank."

"More of John Heartless's decisions," said Jimmy, shaking his head sadly.

By the time they pulled up in front of the bank, it was almost dark outside. They looked up at a steel gray, granite building. Its straight sides shot up to the sky; the top of the building almost poking into the clouds.

"Bernard, will you stay back with me?" asked Randy. "I don't want to be alone if John Heartless shows up."

"Sounds fine to me," said Bernard, looking to Jimmy, Jamal, and Lilly.

"No problem," said Jimmy, Jamal, and Lilly together.

Jimmy, Jamal, and Lilly climbed up many steps to get to the large front door. Near the top step, Jamal walked over to one of the fierce-looking stone lions that sat on either side of the door. "Good, kitty," said Jamal, patting the stone lion's head.

Suddenly, the lion's head began to kind of melt. It then reshaped into a man's head. It was a man with a crown and a sinister black goatee.

"It's John Heartless!" cried Jamal with a shriek, taking two steps back. "Welcome to my bank," said the head sweetly. Then the smile turned into a sneer. "Take care of business, and be on your way—fast!" Then in a blink, the head turned once more into a growling lion.

Jamal stood there frozen, not saying a word.

"C'mon, Jamal," said Jimmy. "Give me a hand with this door. It's too heavy for just one person to pull."

Together, Jamal and Jimmy began to pull open the big front door of the bank. "I wish I was home. I wish I was home," said Jamal over and over. "I'd even clean my room if I could just be back at home."

Their footsteps echoed loudly as they walked into the huge, cold, gray marble room. Lilly pointed up to the domed ceiling. "Wow, this actually is very cool. Look at the different locations in Sweet Abundance painted right on the ceiling."

"What is your business?" called the teller from across the room.

Jimmy walked to the teller station followed by his companions. "I want to cash my one-hundred-dollar inheritance card," said Jimmy, sliding the card across the counter to the teller.

The teller looked at the card. He pulled out a drawer next to him and took out a one-hundred-dollar bill and handed it to Jimmy. "Now you must leave immediately. It's for your own good." The teller started to look around uncomfortably. He took out a white handkerchief and began dabbing the sweat off his face.

"I need to use the bathroom," said Jimmy calmly. "Can you tell me where it is?"

The teller pointed across the huge room. "It's over there. But hurry!"

"But Jimmy . . . we just stopped . . . and . . ." Jamal started.

"You guys wait over there," said Jimmy, pointing to some chairs along the wall. "I'll be right out."

"You will?" asked Jamal, his eyes opened wide with concern.

Lilly stared at her brother. Her eyes narrowed as she tried to figure out what Jimmy was doing. "C'mon, Jamal," said Lilly. "If he says he'll be right out then he will be right out. We have to trust that he knows what he is doing. That's right, Jimmy, isn't it?"

"I promise," answered Jimmy, smiling at his sister for the first time in a long while. He then walked quickly over to the men's room door. But before the door closed, Jamal and Lilly could see him open the guide book that he had brought from the basement of Otto's store.

It was only five minutes before the door opened again with a bang. "Oh no!" screamed Jamal, putting his hands on his face.

Lilly walked over to the tall man in the black cape who had walked out in Jimmy's place. Her face was red, her mouth was a straight line, and her hands were on her hips.

"What have you done with my brother?" Lilly asked. Her voice was hard, and her eyes were as cold as ice. "You better not have hurt him even one little bit."

Jamal popped two mini-bites. "OK . . . We're dead now."

"You were told to leave immediately," said John Heartless, snarling. "Now I'm afraid you have waited too long. Your brother is safe for now . . . come with me." Then just like at Make Your Fortune John Heartless ushered them to a door marked: Office. Once they were in the office, John Heartless closed the door and turned the lock on the knob.

Jamal started to cry. "Please don't hurt us!" he wailed. "All I want to do is go home!"

"C'mon, Jamal. Stop your blubbering," said Jimmy's voice.

Lilly and Jamal looked around the room, but there was no sign of Jimmy. Just then, John Heartless took off his crown, and his head got all quivery like the stone lion's head. Soon, they were looking at John Heartless with Jimmy's head.

"I have no time to explain," said Jimmy's head. "Let's get busy looking for the pens."

He put the crown back on his head, and in seconds they were looking at John Heartless—or whoever he was.

They looked in all the drawers, in the large desk in front of the large picture window—no luck finding the pens.

"Hey, maybe there is a safe behind this picture on the wall," suggested Jamal. He lifted the picture. "Oh, Phooey, there's no safe here."

"Check under the carpet for a trap door," suggested Jimmy.

"Nope, no trap door," said Lilly.

"What are we going to do?" asked Lilly. "The real John Heartless will show up here any second."

"We need to think," said Jimmy. "Think about the clue that Isadore gave me. The pens are to be found where John Heartless would never set foot."

Lilly began to pace back and forth trying to think of a place in a bank that John Heartless would not set foot. Jamal followed behind her. They were walking back and forth like a little parade.

Jimmy was turning around slowly in the large leather swivel chair behind the desk. "Wait!" said Jimmy. "I think I've got it."

"Got what?" asked Jamal.

Jamal and Lilly ran over to the desk as Jimmy began searching through the top desk drawer. "I know. I saw them in here," said Jimmy.

"You mean you saw the pens?" asked Lilly.

"No, I didn't find the pens. Oh, here it is," said Jimmy, holding up an old ring of keys.

Suddenly, they heard a banging on the door. "Unlock this door at once—you little punks, or I'll break it down."

"OK...OK..." said Jimmy "I'm coming."

Jimmy handed the ring of keys to Jamal who was standing right next to him. He motioned for Jamal to put them in his pocket. Then Jimmy took off his crown and began turning back into Jimmy.

"Wait a second," Jimmy said through the door as he continued to change. "I can't get this lock unstuck."

Finally, Jimmy stood there as himself. The only thing left of his John Heartless disguise was the crown token in his hand.

"You brats have exactly thirty seconds to open the door, or I'll break it down!" John Heartless was screaming now.

Jimmy opened the door, and John Heartless grabbed Jimmy by the collar. "You are all going to join Isadore in Dead End!" John Heartless was still screaming.

Lilly and Jamal followed John Heartless and Jimmy out of the bank, down the steps, and over to John Heartless's long black limo.

"We are going for a ride," said John Heartless with a snarl. He opened the door of the long black limousine. What he wasn't expecting, though, was a little wiener dog to come flying out of the car right into his face.

"Hey! What in the world!" John Heartless jumped back in surprise...and let go of Jimmy's collar.

Jimmy, Lilly, and Jamal all started running to their friend Randy, whose engine was already humming.

Bernard barked and snarled at John Heartless and then finally made a run for it. When he reached the van, he took a giant leap and landed right in Jamal's lap. Jamal shut the door as Randy's tires squealed. They were heading off down the path—away from the bank.

John Heartless stretched out his arm like a rubber band. "You can't get away so fast!" He laughed his most evil laugh as his hand reached for the van and began pulling it backward to the bank.

Randy spun his wheels, trying to get loose from John Heartless's grip. Randy tried and tried to move forward and take them to safety, but John Heartless was too strong for the little van. Randy began going backwards—closer and closer to the evil John Heartless.

Then, the most surprising thing happened. Jamal, chicken of the world, the biggest baby you could ever know, chocolate, mini-bite-popping Jamal leaned himself out the window, opened his mouth, and bit down on John Heartless's hand as hard as he could!

"Jamal!" shouted Lilly. "I don't believe you just did that!"

"Ouch!" screamed John Heartless and let go of the van.

Then Randy took off like a shot. "Yippee!" shouted Jamal. "You are really speedy!"

As they raced away, they could still hear John Heartless screaming, "I'll get all of you yet—you little creeps! I'll get you yet!"

"Way to go, Jamal," called Jimmy. "I knew you had bravery in you all the time."

"Yeah, I guess I'm braver than I thought," said Jamal, holding on to Bernard for dear life.

"OK, Jimmy," said Lilly, trying to be a little bit in charge. "What's with the keys?"

Chapter 8

JIMMY SMILED. "THIS whole key thing is actually pretty cool. Remember how Isadore said that the pens were in a place where John Heartless would never set foot. I tried to think of a place that stands for good things like fun and imagination and learning about the past and present. It would be a place that is opposite of everything that John Heartless stands for."

"You mean like the zoo?" asked Jamal.

"Something like that," answered Jimmy.

"What you're saying is all fine and good," said Lilly, trying hard to be patient. "But nothing you said explains the keys."

"Jamal, take out the keys, please," said Jimmy.

Jamal took the ring of keys out of his pocket and held them up for everyone to see. There, hanging from the ring along with the golden letter I, were three old-fashioned skeleton keys.

"These are obviously Isadore's keys," said Jimmy, taking the keys from Jamal and holding up the golden letter I. I'm counting on one of these keys to open the door to the place where John Heartless won't go—to the place where the pens are hidden.

"What place?" asked Lilly with no patience left in her voice.

"Yeah, what place and where is it?" asked Jamal.

"If my hunch is right, the place should be on Schoolhouse Street," said Jimmy.

"That's the street next to the Dead End," added Lilly.

"You'll know it the minute you see it," answered Jimmy, grinning.

Randy continued at top speed. "John Heartless isn't far behind," said Randy. "I can almost feel him behind us."

Chapter 9

THE PATH AWAY from the bank wound around like a snake. There were many exit paths, but Randy ignored them and kept right on going.

"I hope you know what you are doing, Randy," said Lilly as they flew past another exit.

"Here is the right one now!" said Randy and made a sharp turn off the main path.

"Whoa!" said all the passengers as they leaned together to one side.

They looked up at the exit sign that said, "Schoolhouse Avenue." Soon they were flying down the exit ramp.

"Any sign of John Heartless?" asked Jimmy, keeping his eye on the road ahead.

Lilly, Jamal, and Bernard all looked behind them. "No sign of him," they all answered.

"Where could he be?" asked Jimmy. But no one had an answer.

"Hey! There's the Dead End!" cried Jamal. "It's there at the end of the street."

"We're not going to the Dead End yet," said Jimmy, and he turned Randy down the Dead End access road that went around the Dead End.

"I can see Isadore's face in the little window of the Dead End," said Lilly. She waved and so did Jimmy and Jamal just in case he could see them.

Randy slowed down, as Jimmy lightly pushed down on the brake and turned down Schoolhouse Street. "We should see the place on this street," said Jimmy.

Everyone looked at each house carefully as they drove down the street. Lilly kept looking behind for John Heartless. He had to be close behind.

Suddenly, Jimmy slammed on the brakes. "Ouch!" hollered Randy. "Not so hard on the brakes. All you had to do is tell me to stop."

"I'm really sorry," said Jimmy, opening the van door. "But . . . everyone . . . look at that building!"

Lilly, Jamal, Bernard, and Randy looked at the old white building with green shutters. They jumped out of the van and followed Jimmy up the path toward the building. Lilly put her hands over her mouth in surprise. "Oh my gosh," she said in a whisper.

"Are my eyes playing tricks on me?" said Jamal. "It's the children's museum—a cartoon children's museum! It's even got the sign that your Mom hung next to the front door."

"What's the children's museum?" asked Bernard, racing to catch up.

"Schoolhouse Street—an old school—children's museum—stands for fun and imagination—last place John Heartless would go. Very clever thinking, Isadore," said Jimmy smiling.

Jimmy took the keys out of his pocket. He carefully put one of the keys in the lock on the front door. He tried to turn it a few times, but it didn't work. Then he tried the second of the three keys, and it went in easily but just wouldn't turn all the way.

"Oh boy," said Lilly, looking at Jimmy. "Let's hope the third key will be the one."

The third key was an identical copy of the two other keys. Jamal popped two mini-bites. Jimmy polished the key on his sleeve then slowly inserted the key in the lock. "Please be the one," whispered Jimmy. Slowly he turned the key. Click . . . click . . . click, and the door was open.

They had no time for sighs of relief or cheering. They just shoved the door open.

Chapter 10

THEY ALL GASPED as they stood inside the door. "Can this be true?" asked Jamal, rubbing his eyes.

"This is exactly how the inside of the museum looks," said Lilly, not really believing what she was seeing. "It is exactly the way we left it this afternoon."

Jimmy went over to the wooden crate, took out the beautiful mahogany box with the words "The Game" written in fancy curlicue letters. He then removed the top with the game board inlaid in gold, just as he had done earlier that day. He reached in and took out the red and yellow cards and put them on the board in their proper places.

"Geeze, Jimmy!" Jamal complained. "There is no time for us to play The Game now."

"I won't play long. I'll just play until I pick a red card," Jimmy replied.

"Just pick one," said Lilly, nervously looking out the window.

"It won't work if you're not actually playing The Game," said Jimmy.

Jimmy rolled the dice, and it was an eight. "That would be the box to pick a red card," he said. He did not even take the crown token out of his pocket. Jimmy just picked the top card. "Take the money. It's for a good cause," Jimmy read.

"What money?" Jamal asked. "I'm definitely not going back to that bank! That is for sure!"

Lilly tapped Jimmy on the shoulder and said softly, "Maybe you're supposed to take the money from The Game."

Jimmy looked at her for a second and then began to take the money out of the drawer of the beautiful mahogany box and put it in his visitor's bag.

"We still haven't found the pens," said Jamal, running to the window for a look.

"Let's start looking," said Jimmy.

They went through boxes and closets. Jamal even lifted a rug from the floor, looking for a trap door. No pens.

"Where would someone hide pens?" asked Jimmy out loud.

Jamal called from the office in the back. "Hey, guys, come back here."

Jimmy, Lilly, and Bernard ran back to Dad's office. Jamal was standing behind the desk holding a pencil can in his hand.

"Oh my goodness," said Lilly. "That was the pencil can that I made for Dad when I was in second grade. See the stars I put on it. Wow, how did Isadore know to add this?"

Jamal pulled out three pens that were made of shiny metal. "Check this out," said Jamal, holding them up. "The colors of the pens keep on changing."

"That is so cool," said Lilly. "They look like an ever-changing rainbow."

"Those have to be them," said Jimmy. "Let's give them a test."

Jimmy took a greenish metal pen (that was changing to red) from Jamal. He took the cap off the pen, which looked like a cat's-eye marble. Next, he drew a stick figure of a boy and a girl on the large desk calendar that covered a large part of the desk. Everyone gathered around and waited for something to happen but nothing did.

"I guess I was wrong," said Jimmy and snapped the marble cap back on the pen.

As soon as the marble cap was back in place, the two stick figures lifted off the page and stood up on the top of the desk. The boy figure took the girl's hand. "Thanks," said a squeaky voice. Then they jumped off the desk and ran out the back door.

Jimmy, Lilly, and Jamal looked at each other. "That's them," they all chimed in together.

"We don't want John Heartless to get his hands on these pens," said Lilly.

"We've got to hide them until we get them to Isadore. You know John Heartless is going to catch up with us soon."

"Maybe the answer is in here," said Jimmy, as he was thumbing through the guide book.

"Do we really have time for this?" said Lilly impatiently. "Forget hiding them. Let's just run over to the Dead End before John Heartless gets here. We'll give them to Isadore and then everything will be fine."

"Wait . . . wait . . . I think I found it," said Jimmy, smiling. He ran his finger under some words as he read them to himself.

"Hurry!" Jamal yelled. "I can see John Heartless's car coming down the street."

"Randy! Quick! Drive around behind the museum!" Lilly called out the front door.

In a flash, Randy was up the driveway and around the back of the museum.

Jamal and Lilly watched as John Heartless's car came slowly down the street. Did he see Randy?" asked Jimmy as he was taking the marble cap off one of the pens.

"I'm not sure," said Jamal. "What are you doing?"

Jimmy was sitting at the desk drawing a picture of a drawstring bag. On the front of the bag, he printed the word "marbles." Lilly and Jamal just watched as Jimmy snapped the cap back on the pen and lifted the bag up off the paper. Next, he drew a large circle on the paper and placed the pens in the center. "Wait till you see this," said Jimmy. "At least if it works like the guide book says."

Lilly and Jamal watched as Jimmy pulled the cat's-eye marble cap off the orange pen turning green. "What's it supposed to do?" asked Jamal.

"It's a type of eraser. At least that is what the guide book says," answered Jimmy. "Let's see if it works."

Jimmy held the special marble about an inch above the pens and moved it back and forth. "Whoa!" said Jamal. "They're disappearing! The pens are actually being erased. I don't believe my eyes."

"This is so cool," said Jimmy. "And look, see the colorful, tiny marbles that are forming. They are the eraser crumbs."

"This is completely awesome," said Lilly, touching the little marbles with her fingertips. "I think there is every color imaginable here."

Jimmy carefully picked up the tiny marbles, including the cat's-eye eraser marble and put them in the draw-string bag; pulling the strings tightly. Then Jimmy stuffed the bag in his pocket.

They all ran out the back door. Randy was waiting with the motor running. The little van pulled slowly out of the driveway. "Look up there," said Jimmy. "John Heartless's car is way up the street. He went right past the museum."

Jimmy, Lilly, and Jamal held their breath as Randy turned quietly onto the access road toward the Dead End. When they pulled up to the Dead End, they saw the smiling face of Isadore waiting for them in the window, his mustache perfectly curled over each cheek.

They jumped out of the car and ran to the small building. "Boy, oh boy, this is really working out great!" said Lilly happily.

They stopped in their tracks when they heard the squeal of breaks. No one wanted to turn around. They knew John Heartless's long black car had arrived.

"Going to the Dead End to visit your old friend?" said John Heartless in a sickeningly sweet voice as he stepped out of the limo. "Maybe you brought him a present—maybe some pens. That would make a nice gift."

Jimmy looked him right in the eye. "Nope—no pens. We just came to say good-bye. We're going home."

Chapter 11

JOHN HEARTLESS'S FACE turned tomato red, and his neck stretched straight up so that he was the height of a large tree. "Give me those pens!" he bellowed.

Jimmy emptied his pockets. "All I have is my token, some money from The Game, a bag of marbles, my visitor's bag, and the little statue I got from Otto's store. The little statue was supposed to be a surprise for Isadore," said Jimmy quietly.

John Heartless grabbed Jimmy and held him by the feet so he would hang upside down. Nothing fell out of his pockets. "Rats!" he yelled and put Jimmy down.

Still angry, John Heartless grabbed the visitor's bag and dumped everything on the ground. Jimmy stood silently looking at the money he had taken from beautiful mahogany box from The Game. It was scattered all over the sidewalk.

"What about the bag of marbles? Did you hide the pens in there?" said John Heartless, as he dumped out the tiny marbles on the sidewalk just like he dumped the money from The Game. "Nothing but marbles," he said angrily and threw down the empty marble bag.

"What about you two?" John Heartless growled. Then he spun around, looking at Lilly and Jamal. Lilly and Jamal quickly emptied their pockets. Lilly emptied her visitor's bag on the sidewalk along with chewing gum, a small nail file, and a bottle of pink sparkle nail polish.

Jamal emptied his visitor's bag down on the sidewalk too, along with the last two mini-bite candies. "You never know when you might need a snack," said Jamal, trying to smile at John Heartless.

"Who cares about your stupid candy!" roared John Heartless. "I want those pens!"

Jimmy, Jamal, and Lilly quickly picked up their belongings off the sidewalk and put them back in their pockets.

John Heartless stood staring hard at Jimmy. "Drat!" he snarled, twirling his mustache. "You've got those pens. I just know it."

"It says in the guide book that we are allowed to visit the Dead End," said Jimmy quietly.

"You've got five minutes," said John Heartless coldly. "And I will be waiting outside. I'll decide what to do with you then. That is unless you can show me where the pens are hidden."

"Sorry," said Jimmy as he led the way around the side of the Dead End building to a door marked: Visiting Room.

They walked into a plain room with no windows. In the middle of the room was a simple wooden table with chairs all around it. There was nothing on the wall except a picture of the villain they had just left outside. Lilly looked a second time at the picture on the wall and saw the eyes blink.

Casually leaning over to Jimmy, Lilly whispered in Jimmy's ear. "Whatever you do, *don't* turn around and look at the picture on the wall. I just saw the eyes blink." Jimmy simply nodded his head and kept looking forward.

Jimmy went over and knocked on the door. "Isadore," Jimmy called.

Isadore opened the door, walked in, and sat down at the table. It was like looking at a younger version of Otto. Jimmy sat down in the chair opposite him. "So glad you are finally here," said Isadore.

Jamal looked over at the door that led to the outside and then to the door that Isadore had just walked through. "None of the doors are locked," he said to Isadore. "I thought you were stuck here and couldn't get out. I don't get it."

"It is a place with rules," said Isadore kindly. "And I play by them. If you end up in Dead End then you do not leave until someone brings you a Dead End Rescue Card. Did you bring a Dead End Rescue Card with you?"

"They all seem to be missing," said Jimmy sadly.

An evil giggle, so soft that it could barely be heard came from somewhere behind the picture on the wall but neither Jimmy nor Isadore said a word.

"This is my sister Lilly," said Jimmy, pointing to Lilly. "And this is my best friend Jamal."

Jamal walked over and shook Isadore's hand. "Nice to meet you, sir," said Jamal. And then, by sheer luck, Jamal walked over to the wall where John Heartless's picture hung and stood right in front of it. He had no idea that he was blocking the view of the man standing behind the picture.

"Nice to meet you too," said Isadore, not looking at Jamal and Lilly but staring hard at Jimmy. "I'm glad to have some visitors. I hope you have enjoyed your visit to Sweet Abundance."

"It's been interesting, Isadore," said Jimmy, staring back at Isadore. "But we really must go home now. We came to say good-bye." Then Jimmy took the little statue that looked just like Isadore out of his pocket. "Here, this statue is a little present I brought for you."

"Thank you, Jimmy," said Isadore. He had a confused look on his face. He searched Jimmy's face, trying to figure out what the little statue was all about.

"I brought it from Otto's store. I was reading in the guide book, and I thought you might enjoy having it," said Jimmy, never taking his eyes away from Isadore.

Suddenly a light bulb appeared for a few seconds above Isadore's head. "Yes, yes," he said, now smiling as he took the statue from Jimmy. "This will bring me much enjoyment." He got up from the chair. "I'll put this away with my things."

"How are we getting home?" asked Jamal, chewing happily on a mini-bite. "Gee, I wonder what Mom is making for dinner?"

"I'm still working on that," said Jimmy quietly.

Jamal stopped chewing. His eyes got big. "Oh, you mean John Heartless. Yeah, we gotta get past old John Heartless—don't we? Well, don't worry. I won't let him give us any trouble. I showed him before, didn't I?"

Neither Jimmy nor Lilly could tell Jamal to be quiet. They looked at each other; both shaking their heads. Both understood what that meant. They couldn't let Jamal know that John Heartless was hiding right behind him. So they let him chatter on until Isadore came back to the room.

Isadore walked in carrying the little statue. "You know, kids. I think I will be getting out soon myself, and I will have a lot to carry. Do you think you could take this statue to the children's museum on Schoolhouse Street for me?" he said, handing the statue to Jimmy.

"The children's museum!" boomed a voice behind the picture on the wall. Poor Jamal jumped a foot at the unexpected voice and fainted right on the spot.

Chapter 12

IN A FLASH, John Heartless was at the door. He grabbed Isadore by the collar. "You're not going anywhere so fast!" he sneered.

Lilly knelt next to Jamal, tapping his cheeks like they do in the movies to wake someone up. Finally, his eyes fluttered open. "Are we home?" he asked.

"No," said Lilly kindly as she helped him up. "Not yet."

John Heartless shoved Jimmy, Lilly, and Jamal out the door to his limo. "Now get in!" he screeched. He bent over and looked into the car to make sure there was no dog ready to jump out.

Lilly looked over her shoulder before getting into the long scary limo. She saw Isadore's face in the window. "Hey, Isadore!" she called to him, but he didn't reply. He was just looking straight ahead. Isadore didn't look scared or mad. He just stared.

Jimmy, Jamal, and Lilly sat in the back seat of the limo. The seats were smooth leather, and, like the bank, the inside of the car was dark and cold.

"The children's museum on Schoolhouse Street . . . and make it snappy!" ordered John Heartless to the driver.

Jimmy turned around to look out the back window. He silently tapped Lilly and Jamal and pointed so they would look too. Out the window, two cars behind was their faithful van, Randy. Bernard was in the front seat with his front paws propped up on the dashboard looking straight ahead at the limo.

Lilly looked out her window, and in the distance could still see the Dead End building. There was Isadore's face still in the window, still staring straight ahead. She turned to Jimmy who was deep in his own thoughts. *He's probably trying to figure out what to do next, just like I am,* she thought. Lilly turned to Jamal who had his arms wrapped around himself shaking like a leaf.

Lilly could see the top of the marble bag sticking out of Jimmy's pocket. In Jimmy's hand was the little statue of Isadore. *Why had Isadore given the statue back?* Lilly wondered to herself.

Suddenly, the head of the little statue turned and looked straight at Lilly and smiled at her. Lilly gasped. Then, just as suddenly, it froze again like a statue. Lilly sat back in the seat and smiled. *Hmm,* she thought. *It looks like Isadore escaped from Dead End after all. This should be very interesting.*

In the front seat sat John Heartless. "Now I've got you, Isadore," he said out loud. "Now I've got you. Abundance will soon be mine and you can spend forever rotting in Dead End. Heh . . . heh . . . heh . . ."

Soon they stopped at the children's museum and John Heartless pulled them roughly out of the long, black limo. Jamal's lip started to quiver and Lilly quickly put her arm around his shoulders. "C'mon Jamal," she said in a whisper. "Everything is going to be OK. You'll see."

"At least I hope so," she said to herself.

"Unlock the door," sneered John Heartless when they were all standing in front of the door of the children's museum.

Jimmy took the keys out of the inside of his shoe where he had hidden them and unlocked the door. John Heartless snatched the keys away from Jimmy and stuck them in his pocket. "Get in there," he said, pushing everyone through the door.

"Now show me where the pens are!" John Heartless bellowed. Jimmy, Lilly, and Jamal just stood there looking at him.

Little puffs of steam came shooting out of his ears. His face turned red, and his eyes bugged out. The crown on his head shot straight up in the air before returning to his head with a thud."

John Heartless took three wooden chairs and lined them up next to each other. "Sit down," he ordered. He took the rope from around a large crate and wound it around Jimmy's wrist and then the chair. "So much for your little present for Isadore," he said and threw it across the room where it landed on an old chair upholstered in red and blue flowered fabric. It was a worn old chair that was torn in several places with the stuffing hanging out.

"You two are next," John Heartless growled.

"We didn't do anything wrong," said Jamal sadly, his lips quivering.

Ignoring Jamal's words, John Heartless tied up Lilly and Jamal just as he had tied up Jimmy.

Jimmy looked down silently to study the knots that tied him up. Lilly sat frozen and furious. Jamal began to wail, "I want to go home!" Tears poured down his round cheeks, and he began to shake.

"Just tell me where the pens are, and I will send you home right away," said John Heartless softly, smiling his evil smile.

Jamal looked at Lilly and Jimmy. Lilly glared at him. Jimmy just smiled at him.

"Well," Jamal started.

"I think the pens might be in the basement," Lilly blurted out. "I'm not sure though."

John Heartless stretched his neck and practically put his nose on Lilly's nose. "Thank you, young lady. For your sake, they better be down there," he growled. His head popped back in place, and he made a dash for the basement stairs.

"Whew!" said Lilly wrinkling her nose. "His breath smells like stinky garbage. It makes you want to throw up."

"Now what to do we do?" asked Jamal.

"Let me think for a minute," said Jimmy. "I'm trying to figure out these knots."

After a few minutes of silence, Lilly whispered, "Did you hear that?"

"Hear what?" asked Jamal also in a whisper.

"I heard it again," said Lilly softly. She looked over at Jimmy who had his head tilted to one side listening. "You heard it too, didn't you?"

"Shhh," said Jimmy, trying harder to listen. "Wait! I think I heard some words."

Then they all heard the voice. It was still very soft, but this time they were all able to hear the words clearly. "Spit on me."

They weren't able to hear any more because of the crashing sounds coming from the basement. "That lousy John Heartless is throwing around our father's precious museum stuff, just so he can find those pens," said Lilly, wishing she could jump out of her chair and tell him what she thought of him.

"Lilly, you've got a light bulb floating above your head," said Jimmy.

Lilly looked up and there it was. Then *poof*, the light bulb disappeared, but the idea stayed just fine in her head.

That is when she told Jimmy and Jamal about what had happened in the limo. "The little statue turned its head and smiled at me," she said, finishing her story.

"That's how Isadore got out of Dead End," said Jimmy. "The statue is back at the Dead End staring out the window. So just like Jamal spit on Randy and Bernard, we must now spit on the little statue."

"Which is across the room at the moment, where we can't get to him," Jamal pointed out.

When the crashing in the basement started again, Jimmy started to make his chair hop closer to Lilly. "Good idea," said Jamal, and he started hopping his chair close to Lilly too.

"Maybe we can help each other get untied," said Jimmy.

With all the crashing noise in the basement and the chair hopping noise, they didn't hear Bernard push the back door open and trot over to where they were. "What's happening?" called Bernard above the racket.

"Oh, Bernard, Bernard!" cried Jamal. "I'm so happy to see you boy."

"Really?" said Bernard and ran over to Jamal, jumped on his lap and started to lick Jamal's face.

"Bernard," called Jimmy.

Bernard turned his head, jumped off Jamal's lap, and went over to Jimmy; his tail wagging a mile a minute.

"There is a little statue of Isadore on that chair over there across the room. Will you go and get it please?" said Jimmy.

"Sure, no problem," said Bernard, trotting across the room.

Bernard ran across the room and jumped up on the chair. He picked up the statue gently in his teeth and ran straight to Jimmy. At least he tried to run straight to Jimmy. Halfway there, he ran into two legs in black pants. "What have we here?" said a growling voice as John Heartless reached down and pulled the little statue out of Bernard's mouth. Bernard quickly dashed away, so there would be no chance of being grabbed.

John Heartless held the little statue in his hand and examined it carefully. "This little statue seems awfully important to you. I wonder if it is hollow. Maybe if I smash it to pieces, we can see what is inside."

Jimmy, Lilly, and Jamal all looked at each other. "We're doomed!" wailed Jamal.

"Don't you dare smash that!" said Lilly. Her mouth was an angry frown, and her red curls quivered. "It belongs to Isadore. We brought it for him as a present."

"It doesn't belong to him anymore," said John Heartless. "Finders . . . keepers . . . losers . . . weepers. So there." He headed toward the back door so he could smash the statue outside.

Lilly's eyes began to fill with tears just thinking about being in Dead End for the rest of her life. Then Jamal once again began to sob and shake.

Bernard poked his head around the old, raggedy chair. He tilted his head when he saw Jamal sobbing. Then without another thought, the little dachshund made a run for Jamal.

Bernard scampered across the room toward Jamal but didn't quite make it. Halfway there, he ran right in front of John Heartless who was too busy examining the statue to notice the little dachshund crossing his path.

Jimmy, Lilly, and Jamal watched in shock as John Heartless took a step and tripped over Bernard. John Heartless flew up nearly a foot with his arm straight out in front of him. His hand opened and out flew the little statue.

"Jimmy, do you think the statue will land in your hands?" whispered Jamal, as he watched it fly through the air.

"No," Jimmy whispered back to Jamal. "It's going right over my head. It's going right into . . . oh no . . . my Dad's fish tank." The statue landed right in the tank with barely a splash.

John Heartless got up. His face was bright red for the second time that day. "Where is that little runt of a dog?" he screamed.

John Heartless looked around angrily for Bernard who had made a dash out the back door. "Don't you even think about moving a muscle," said John Heartless, as he made his way out the back door.

The back door closed behind him. His crown bobbed in front of the window as he chased after Bernard. "I'll get you, you little mutt!" Two minutes later, the crown went bobbing back in the opposite direction.

"We have no time to waste," said Jimmy. He hopped his chair even closer to Lilly. "See if you can untie my wrists."

Lilly tried reaching over to untie Jimmy. "Sorry, Jimmy," said Lilly. "The knots won't budge."

Chapter 13

THAT IS WHEN they heard a bubbling sound coming from the fish tank. "I can't believe my eyes!" said Jamal. "The statue is starting to grow. This is so much better than spitting on it."

"Please don't let Dad's fish tank get ruined," said Lilly. "He loves that tank and his fish so much."

Soon the figure was about one foot tall. Then, when it was a little taller, it hopped out. "Thank goodness," said Lilly with relief. "Look, the fish are swimming around as happy as can be."

Again, they saw the crown bob quickly past the back window. Isadore got bigger with each step, and by the time he got to the chairs where Jimmy, Jamal, and Lilly were sitting, he was full size. "Thank you," he said kindly.

"But who is sitting in the Dead End's window?" asked Jamal.

"Why, the statue of course," said Isadore with a little chuckle, as he quickly untied the ropes. "I'd take the time to explain, but we have no time to lose. John Heartless will be back any minute."

"The pens are in my marble bag," said Jimmy.

"Oh, so you erased them. Good thinking, young man." With that Isadore took the marble bag from Jimmy. "Everything will be fine now."

"Fine for me!" screeched John Heartless, running into the room. His crown was a little off center, and there was a large tear in his right pant leg. Trapped under his arm was Bernard, wiggling around furiously to get loose. John Heartless reached over with the other arm and grabbed the bag of marbles out of Isadore's hands. "Now I've got no use for any of you! You are all history! Abundance is mine."

Lilly looked over at Jamal, waiting for his tears to start, but instead she saw Jimmy's eyes get red and fill with tears. "You better not even think about touching my brother or my friend Jamal," Lilly said while glaring full power at John Heartless.

John Heartless stretched his neck over to Lilly, and for the second time, they were nose-to-nose.

"Oh yeah, what are you going to do about it?" John Heartless sneered and then laughed an evil little laugh.

What am I going to do about it? Lilly thought. *I'd really like to punch him and jump up and down on him until he is as flat as a pancake . . . Yeah, like that could really happen! Now wait a minute . . . What about*

Isadore's clue? Look for the last place a man like John Heartless would ever set foot. It turns out to be a place that is about what is good in people.

"Lilly, you've got another light bulb above your head," called Jamal.

"I know," she said, looking up. "I've been trying to figure out what to do and now I think I know. So here it goes—like it or not."

So right then, Lilly held her breath, leaned over, and gave John Heartless a kiss—right on the cheek. John Heartless did not strike back. He put both hands on his cheek. This set Bernard free, and he made a run for Jamal.

"Doesn't he ever brush his teeth?" Lilly said, walking away and rolling her eyes. Both Jimmy and Jamal gasped.

John Heartless stood kind of frozen on the spot; his eyes got as big as saucers. "Ohh . . ." he moaned like he was sick. "You kissed me. I don't remember anyone ever kissing me."

And then he began to shrink.

"He's melting!" Jamal shouted. "Good! We're almost rid of him."

But he didn't melt. He just got smaller. Soon a little boy of about five or six stood in his place.

"Look," Lilly said. "He has the biggest, saddest, darkest brown eyes I have ever seen."

"I want my Mommy and Daddy," said "little John Heartless" and ran over to Lilly, throwing his arms around her. Looking completely confused, Lilly patted his head, looking at Isadore for some help.

"His parents were killed in a train accident when he was a child," said Isadore quietly.

"Please don't send me to my mean old aunt," wailed the little John Heartless. "She hates me." He tightened his arms around Lilly. Tears filled Lilly's eyes as she put her arms around him.

Isadore walked over to the little boy and said in the kindest of voices, "Come with me, little Johnny. I'll take good care of you."

Little Johnny let go of Lilly and turned to Isadore. Getting down on one knee, Isadore took the sobbing child into his arms. "Everything is going to be OK now. You'll see," said Isadore in a quiet, patient voice. "All you need is a little love."

"Excuse me," said Jamal. "But do you know how to get us home?"

"Come with me," said Isadore, standing up and taking little Johnny's hand. "I'm going to send you home."

Hand in hand Isadore and little Johnny walked out of the front door of the children's museum. Jimmy picked up the bag of marbles and followed Isadore and little Johnny. Jamal, Lilly, and Bernard followed right behind.

"Hey! Looks like everything is settled now," said Randy cheerfully as the little van saw everyone walking down the front steps of the children's museum.

"We're going home," called Jamal and jumped up in the air with arms wide open. "Hooray!"

"Oh," said Randy sadly. "I guess there will be no more use for me."

Again, Isadore came to the rescue. "Of course you'll be needed. Johnny and I will need you to drive us around Sweet Abundance. Isn't that right, Johnny?"

Little Johnny nodded his head "yes," never once taking his eyes off Isadore.

"You mean I'm not going back to being a token?" said Randy and drove around in a happy little circle.

"You're not but I probably will," said Bernard softly. He looked up at Jamal with sad brown eyes. "It sure was great to be your dog!"

Jamal picked him up and the little dachshund started licking his face. "Can he come home with me?" asked Jamal.

"Jamal, don't forget that your parents are allergic to dogs," said Lilly in her best in-charge voice. But then in a new, softer, kinder voice, she added smiling. "Although you couldn't ask for a better dog."

"I know a little boy who could really use a friendly dog," said Isadore.

All eyes turned toward little Johnny who was sitting quietly on the grass. Bernard trotted over to the little boy, who only minutes ago had been a horrible villain, ready to get rid of all of them.

The little boy reached out to Bernard and pulled him on his lap. Bernard looked to Jamal and tilted his head to one side. "Go ahead, boy," said Jamal, giving him a thumbs up.

So the little dog started doing what little dogs do best. He started licking the face of his new master. Little Johnny smiled and giggled more and more with each lick.

"Thank you, Jamal," said little Johnny. Then he did what any little boy would do. He lay down so Bernard could jump all over him.

Jimmy walked over to Isadore and handed him the bag of marbles. "Here, these belong to you."

Isadore took a handful of marbles out of the bag. One was a marble eraser. "Here we go," said Isadore as he used the eraser to turn the marbles back into a pen.

The pen was half red and turning a gleaming purple. "Here, this is for you," he said to Jimmy. "Take it, and keep it safe. You just never know when or if you will ever need it."

"It will be safe with me," said Jimmy, putting it carefully in his pants pocket.

"He's right, Isadore," said Lilly. "Knowing my brother, the pen couldn't be in a safer place."

Isadore walked over to Lilly. He took her hand and then leaned over and kissed her on the cheek. "Thank you," he said softly. "You saved the day—a kiss for a kiss."

"*I* saved the day?" said Lilly. Her face was almost as red as her curly hair, but this time, she was smiling a great big smile.

"Yes, you," said Isadore. "You used your head and your heart to come up with the kiss that saved the day."

"Now let's get you all home," said Isadore as he began walking back up the path toward the museum. Everyone followed him up the steps to the front door.

"This is where we say good-bye. Your world is on the other side of that door. Thank you for saving Sweet Abundance and my little friend over there."

All eyes turned to see little Johnny chasing Bernard happily around Randy.

"Yeah, well, who is going to save the day for my Dad's children's museum?" asked Lilly.

"Why Lilly, that has been taken care of already," answered Isadore. "You'll see when you get to the other side."

Isadore shook hands with Jimmy and then with Jamal. He turned to Lilly, but instead of shaking his hand, she gave him a great big hug. "We'll miss you and this place," she said kindly.

Isadore chuckled. "Sweet Abundance will always be with you—in your head and in your heart. Now it's time for you all to go."

Jimmy led the way, just as he had done on the way into Sweet Abundance. "Wow! It's our old museum all right." Jimmy stepped through the doorway and went back to his old non-cartoon Jimmy.

Jamal followed, and Lilly was the last one through. "I just want one last peek," said Lilly. She then looked over her shoulder to see Isadore walking down the steps of the museum, back toward little Johnny, Bernard, and Randy.

Then the door was closed, and they were all back to their old world—back in the children's museum.

Chapter 14

"MRS. STONE, WILLIAM Harris here," said Dad, talking on the phone from the back office of the children's museum. "I'm calling to thank the Mayville Flower and Doll Collectors Club for sending in their donation to the children's museum. Yes . . . you are right . . . children are our greatest resource. Yes . . . yes . . . little buds waiting to bloom. Thank you again for your donation . . . good-bye," Click.

"Problem is," he said aloud to himself. "One hundred dollars is a drop in the bucket."

"Wow," said Jamal. "Isadore brought us back here to the museum. And it was before we went to Otto's store."

"Now our parents won't be worried," said Lilly.

"And I won't be late for dinner," Jamal said, smiling.

They walked over to Dad's office. "Hi, Pops," said Jimmy just like he said before going to Sweet Abundance. "You got a donation of one hundred dollars. That's pretty good."

"Yeah, pretty good," Dad said and tousled Jimmy's brown wavy hair.

"But there's nothing to worry about," said Jamal. "The money problems are all fixed, right?"

"No, Jamal," said Dad sadly. "It would take thousands to get us out of trouble."

"You mean you still need at least twenty thousand dollars?" said Lilly very surprised. "I thought it was all taken care of . . ." She ran to the front door. "I've got a few questions for Isadore."

Lilly opened the door expecting to see Sweet Abundance, but what she saw was the regular old front yard of the children's museum. She ran to Jimmy. "Did Isadore break his promise? I can't believe he would do a thing like that."

"Who's Isadore?" Dad asked. "What's this all about? And how do you know about the twenty thousand dollars?"

"We heard you say it under your breath before you left the museum to go to . . ." Jamal started and then slapped his hand over his mouth.

Dad looked over to Lilly. "Well . . . Dad . . . you see, we . . ." Lilly started.

"Lilly, I have a feeling this is one of your long stories," said Dad with a hint of a smile. "But I've got to leave to see Mr. Avery . . ."

"Of the Matterhorn Loan Company," Jamal finished.

"How in the world did you know that?" said Dad to Jamal. "What is going on around here?"

"Wait," said Jimmy. He stuck his hands in his pockets and pulled out the money from The Game that they got in Sweet Abundance. Then he handed it to his Dad. Jamal and Lilly joined in and took the money they acquired in their adventure and added it to the money Jimmy had given to Dad.

"Jimmy, Lilly, and Jamal, I can't use play money from a board game. We wish it could be real. Everybody wishes play money is real at one time or another. You see, kids . . ." Dad stopped talking midsentence. He took a second look at the money that Jimmy, Lilly, and Jamal had given him. He pulled out one of the bills and looked at it very carefully.

"Where did you get this money?" said Dad in a very serious voice.

"It's a very long story," said Jimmy.

"Yeah," said Jamal. "You'll never believe it, Mr. Harris."

"Lilly," said Dad. "You are the eldest. Like it or not, you were the one put in charge to watch your brother. Will you please tell me what is going on? This is a great deal of money and . . ."

Lilly was smiling now, and her eyes sparkled. "Cancel your appointment with Mr. Avery, and I'll explain the whole thing. Well, . . . I'll at least tell you what happened," said Lilly with a little giggle.

"OK," said Dad, walking over to the phone. "I'll make the call and reschedule for tomorrow—just in case I need to meet with him. Let's pull up some chairs around the aquarium. That's a great place to tell a story."

Jimmy, Lilly, and Jamal all looked at the aquarium and then at each other and smiled.

Then, by the soft glow of the aquarium's light, Lilly carefully told the story of their adventure. She told it without rolling her eyes, checking her nails, or popping her gum. Lilly told the story just like her father tells a story—giving careful thought to each detail.

When she finished, Dad got up and checked The Game to look at the secret compartment, the special cards, and the museum token. Then he checked out his precious aquarium for any nicks or cracks from Isadore climbing out.

"So," he said, finally speaking and holding up the bills. "This used to be cartoon money that turned into real money when you walked through that door over there."

"Yes," they all answered together.

"How will I explain this to your mother? She'll never believe your story. I am having a lot of trouble with the story myself. If it wasn't Lilly telling the story, and if I wasn't holding real money in my hands, I wouldn't have believed one word."

"Aren't you happy, Pops?" asked Jimmy. "Isn't this the answer to your prayers?"

"If this money really belongs to me, then I am the happiest man in the world. If it doesn't, then I've got to find out who the owner of this money is and give it back. And then, unfortunately, I will be meeting with Mr. Avery," answered Dad.

"The money really is for you, Dad," said Jimmy. "You'll see."

"I hope you are right Jimmy, but for now, it's getting late, and we need to go home."

So they walked out the door of the museum and down the front steps. When they got to the bottom step, a big blue van pulled up and turned into the driveway.

"It's Otto's van," shouted Jamal. "See the sign on the side of the van."

"Otto's Antiques. We buy and sell," Dad read aloud. "So there really is an Otto's Antiques."

The back doors of the van sprung open and a platform slid out. Otto rolled onto the platform, which lowered him down to the ground. "Hey, Jimmy, Lilly, and Jamal," called Otto as he wheeled himself over to the steps of the children's museum. "I wanted to make sure you were all right."

"Otto," said Jimmy. "This is my Dad, William Harris. Dad, this is Otto."

Dad reached over and shook hands with Otto. "My daughter certainly described you well," said Dad and winked at Lilly.

Lilly's face turned red but this time with pleasure.

"Tell me, Otto, can I believe the story about Sweet Abundance? Do you have a brother Isadore? Is there a John Heartless? Is all this money real?"

Otto smiled a mysterious smile, and his mustache spread out a little more across his face. "Yes, I do have a brother named Isadore. As for John Heartless and Sweet Abundance—well . . . I find that it is often important to take a chance and go ahead and believe in the most unbelievable things."

"And about the money?" asked Dad.

"Is the money real? Yes, it is because it comes from me," answered Otto. "You see, William, we are both in the business of sparking the imagination of children and grown-ups as well. We both keep old things alive and important. So I decided to make a donation to the children's museum from Otto's Antiques."

Dad's eyes widened, and his mouth hung open with surprise. "I'm speechless!" said Dad, as he began wildly shaking hands with Otto.

Finally, Dad found his words but still continued pumping Otto's entire arm up and down. "Otto, I just don't know how to thank you enough. You have saved the day for me, my family, and for the many children who will enjoy and learn from coming to the museum. Thank you . . . thank you so much."

Otto carefully took his hand away from Dad. "It is my pleasure," said Otto.

"If you will excuse me," said Dad, still looking a little dazed. "I have a few phone calls to make." Then without another word, he ran back into the museum.

"Tell me about your adventure," said Otto.

Everyone sat down on the grass as Lilly again began telling the story of the time they spent in Sweet Abundance.

"Don't forget to tell the part about of how I took a bite out of John Heartless. I really saved the day, didn't I?" Jamal added before Lilly finished the story.

"Good," said Otto with a sharp turn of his wheelchair. He began wheeling himself back to the van.

"Hey, Otto," called Jamal. "Is that money really from you?"

"Of course," Otto replied with a quick wink. "Where else would it come from?"

Otto wheeled himself over to the van, rolled onto the lift, which moved him up so he could easily roll into the van. He looked out the driver's window and waved.

"He reminds me of Isadore looking out the window of the Dead End," said Lilly.

"Bye, kids," Otto called out. "Come and visit me any time."

Jamal hopped on his bike. "I'm going home. I don't want to be late for dinner. Mom keeps saying that I have to be brave and try foods like broccoli. I can't wait to show her how brave I am now. I'll be over later."

Lilly and Jimmy looked at each other for a second. Jimmy started walking over to his bike. "I'm going home too. Now you don't have to keep an eye on me, Lilly."

"Well, it certainly wasn't boring, Jimmy. Anyway, everything turned out fine, and I still have time to go to the mall with my friends after dinner," said Lilly.

"Great," said Jimmy. "You'll like that."

"Yes . . . hmmm . . . but before the mall," replied Lilly, smiling, "I think I will stop to see Otto. Maybe he can tell me how Isadore is doing."

The End